THE DANCING MAIDENS

Lindsey Jamieson comes to remote west Cornwall to a new post as live-in tutor to emotionally disturbed Emma, aged six. Soon, however, Lindsey is plunged into a mystery which seems to involve the family. Is Nick, her employer, all he seems to be? Who walks the hill by night, in the shadow of the 'Dancing Maidens'? And why are the villagers so frightened? Lindsey faces many challenges before the mystery is solved and she can find personal happiness.

Books by Janet Thomas
in the Linford Romance Library:

THE TIDES OF TIME
SUMMER SOJOURN

rary at Home Service
mmunity Services
nslow Library, CentreSpace
eaty Centre, High Street
slow TW3 1ES

WORKING IN PARTNERSHIP WITH

	1	2	3	4	5	6	7	8	9
10	342			7905	C25	1116	958	708	
	451		993	364	1795	846	77	3218	
10	786				565	7726		3178	
10	901	7583			9525	6496	BUSSE4		
	861		3073	9744		3169	587	848	
1387	611		9523		9055		3057		
	972	9443		445	6306		7698		
							3457	9798	
							507		
								448	
								1588	

P10-L2061

JANET THOMAS

THE DANCING MAIDENS

Complete and Unabridged

LINFORD
Leicester

First published in Great Britain in 2004

First Linford Edition
published 2005

British Library CIP Data

Thomas, Janet
   The Dancing Maidens.—Large print ed.—
Linford romance library
   1. Love stories
   2. Large type books
   I. Title
   823.9′2 [F]

   ISBN 1–84395–709–4

Published by
F. A. Thorpe (Publishing)
Anstey, Leicestershire

Set by Words & Graphics Ltd.
Anstey, Leicestershire
Printed and bound in Great Britain by
T. J. International Ltd., Padstow, Cornwall

This book is printed on acid-free paper

1

If I knew then what I know now, I don't suppose I would have accepted the job in the first place, but as life is full of choices, I thought at the time I was on to a good thing.

Living-in, big house in the country, miles from anywhere, it seemed the ideal escape from London life just when I needed it most. Which was why I was facing my new employer, Nicholas Penwarne, with a stomach full of butterflies and an expectant smile on my face, delighted that he had taken me on.

'Well, Miss Jamieson,' he was saying when I interrupted.

'Oh, please — call me Lindsey.'

'Right then, Lindsey.' There was no answering smile from him, and the deep cleft between his eyebrows looked as if it could easily become a frown.

He ran a hand absently through his shock of honey-coloured hair, and went on, 'If you are really going to help my daughter, Emma, you'd better know the circumstances of her background right from the beginning.'

He gave me a penetrating look. His eyes were toffee-brown, deep-set, and his brows and lashes were thick and dark. The combination of fair hair and dark eyes was unusual. And very attractive. Early thirties, I guessed, strong jaw-line, straight nose, determined-looking mouth. Then I started taking notice of what he was saying.

'Rachel, my wife, died two years ago, when Emma was four.'

I already knew this much, and that the little girl was emotionally disturbed, but the sudden pain on his face and the harshness of his voice took me by surprise when he said, 'Emma hasn't spoken since.' He looked down at the pen in his hand and a silence fell.

My jaw dropped and the bright smile slid from my face. This was news to me.

The advertisement for the job had only said, 'Companion/Tutor required for emotionally disturbed girl', and the solicitor who interviewed me in London had never mentioned any reasons. I felt a surge of sympathy for this gaunt-faced man, and for the little girl, too.

More so, probably, because I had had my own traumas. That was why I had chosen to come to this remote western tip of Cornwall, hopefully to begin a new life.

'Oh, how dreadful,' I murmured, and the words sounded trite and inadequate.

'Yes,' Nicholas said, and his mouth snapped shut like a trap. 'Now, about Emma.' He straightened his shoulders and met my eyes. 'We have taken her to the best of medical experts and they all say the same thing. That there is nothing physically wrong. Give her time. But it's been two years now, with no sign of improvement. I feel we have waited long enough.'

His eyes bored into mine. 'That's

why I've engaged you, Lindsey, as a professional therapist, to be with her constantly, and see what you can do on a one-to-one basis.'

'Who looks after her at the moment?' I asked. Having only just arrived, I had no idea who else lived in this rambling old house, or in the annex I had seen when the taxi dropped me off. All that registered had been the house, which stood on its own, miles from anywhere, in a landscape of towering granite tors, fringed by the distant sea.

'There are several of us in the family, and our housekeeper lives-in as well. There's always someone around to keep an eye on Emma,' Nicholas replied.

So it seemed she was passed around like a little parcel to whoever was available at the time. Oh yes. 'I suppose she's never actually been to school at all, then? If the tragedy happened when she was four?' I said, still trying to come to grips with this unusual situation.

One little girl in a house full of adults, none of whom was particularly responsible for her. No wonder she wasn't improving. She was probably still deep in the trauma of her mother's death, which any medic should have followed up long ago.

If anyone needed one-to-one treatment, it sounded as if Emma did. Well, I wanted a personal challenge. Perhaps we would be good for each other.

'No, that's another thing. She's not getting the company of other children either. We're rather isolated here.' He sighed and shrugged his broad shoulders. 'But Emma is, or was, a bright child, and she was learning her letters and numbers well when Rachel . . . She was a teacher herself, and Emma was on the verge of reading when . . . But, there we are. You know the position now,' he finished, and rose to his feet.

We had been sitting one each side of his cluttered desk in the equally untidy study. As Nicholas unfolded his long legs and stood up, I was struck by how tall he was. Over six feet and lean with it, he towered over my own five feet four. Dressed in shapeless cords and a baggy sweater, he looked the typical archaeologist he was, a combination of the practical and the academic.

He put out his hand as he said, 'I hope you'll be happy here, Lindsey. I shall certainly feel a lot better knowing that Emma is in your charge.'

I shook the extended hand, which was warm and firm, and replied, 'I'm sure I shall be, and I'll do the very best I can for her.'

His face crinkled into a smile and I caught a glimpse of another man behind the careworn features. The unexpected sweetness of the smile which softened the square jaw and smoothed out the stress lines across his brow, also made Nicholas look years younger and somehow vulnerable. It made me hold on to his hand a fraction longer than necessary.

'I'll get Jane to show you up to your room,' he said, moving towards the door. 'Oh, there you are, Jane,' as he opened it into the corridor, where a plump woman in a print overall and slippers was passing. 'I was just going to call you. This is Miss Jamieson — Jane Harris, our housekeeper,' he indicated.

I smiled and nodded, 'Hello.'

'Take care of her and show her around, will you?'

'Please call me Lindsey,' I said for a second time.

Nicholas, still with his hand on the door-knob added, 'Forgive me if I get back to work now. I have an article to write. I'll see you at dinner, Lindsey. Make sure you ask Jane for anything you need.' His other hand was raking through his already rumpled hair, as if this was a regular habit of his.

As he disappeared into the study, Jane Harris remarked, 'Mr Nicholas don't like being disturbed when he's working. Spends hours in that study, he do — forgets his meals and all if I don't call him.' She turned towards the foot of the stairs and went on, 'This way, if you please, Miss — er — Lindsey. I've took your suitcase up.'

I followed her up two flights of stairs. From the window of the first landing was a spectacular view over windswept moorland to the sea about half a mile away. It was looking cold and grey now, for it was only March, but in the summer it must be glorious.

Jane had reached the top and was pushing open a door. 'This here's your room,' she said as we entered. Her voice burred with a broad Cornish accent. 'The bathroom's just opposite.' She waved a hand to demonstrate. 'Little Emma's room's next door. The rest of the family do sleep down the other end.'

The housekeeper stopped to draw breath and I said, 'It's a lovely room, Jane,' and meant it.

The dressing-table and built-in wardrobe were of stripped pine. The carpet and furnishings were in shades of peach and cream, and flower-sprigged curtains hung at the casement windows. The room was on the corner of the house and had two windows, one giving the same stunning view of the sea as the staircase did. The other faced inland towards tumbling, boulder-strewn heights.

'It were Mrs Rachel's favourite, one time. Before . . . well, before,' Jane Harris replied.

'You live-in as well, don't you?' I asked. I slipped off my shoes and wriggled my toes in the thick peach carpet. It was blissful.

'Yes, I've got a flat in the other wing, down along. Some rambling old place this is. Used to be three farm cottages years ago. Mr Nick's brother, John, and Mrs Amy do live in that there converted barn across the yard, see?' She leaned on the window-sill and pointed to one of the buildings I'd noticed earlier.

'Oh, yes. Tell me some more about the family, Jane. I don't know anything about them.'

I perched on the end of the bed as the woman went on.

'Well, Mr John, he stayed on here after they was married because he do work the farm. What's left of it, any

9

road. Only a few sheep now they got, and chickens and ducks. Then there's Mrs Jessica who's Mr Nick's mother, and another brother, Mr Tim.'

'Goodness,' I said, surprised.

Jane Harris glanced curiously at my case. 'That all you got, is it?' she asked bluntly.

'My trunk's coming in a day or two,' I said to satisfy her, and suddenly a feeling of utter rootlessness swept over me like a flood. All my worldly possessions were in that one trunk and suitcase. I'd ruthlessly stripped the flat before I left, and had thrown out most of my past, consigning it to the dustbin and the local Oxfam shop.

But look forward, not back. Perhaps Emma and I could both help each other climb out of the holes we were in.

'Oh, right,' the housekeeper said cheerfully, 'I'll leave you settle in, then. Dinner's at seven and the dining room is on your left as you come down the stairs.' She crossed the room and closed the door behind her.

'Thanks, Jane.' I took a deep breath. I was exhausted. After a journey of over three hundred miles, wondering whether I was doing the right thing or not, here I was. Out in the back of beyond, with a houseful of strangers to face. Plus the challenge of a disturbed and no doubt hostile, child.

Well, you wanted a change girl, so get on with it I said and slid my feet back into my shoes. The sooner Emma and I were acquainted, the better. There were sounds of movement coming from the room next door, so I would go and visit my small charge right away.

I knocked gently on the half-open door and put my head around it. I saw a large and airy playroom furnished with every toy and pastime any child could wish for. Far too much for one small girl, was my first reaction. It looked as if Emma had been showered with expensive objects to try to make up for the loss of her mother. The room was meticulously tidy, every toy on a shelf, and the boxed games stacked in order of size.

Emma was stretched full-length on the bright rug beside her bed, along with a huge golden Labrador. As I went in she knelt up and flung one arm defensively around the animal's neck. These two looked to be inseparable. I had not bargained for a dog as well, and hesitated before moving forward. It growled at me as I crossed the room, its hackles visibly rising.

I was not at my best with dogs, having had little to do with them, especially large ones like this. I instinctively flinched, and hated myself for doing so, for I knew with a kind of sixth sense that the child would have noticed. Consequently I said over-heartily, 'Hello, Emma, I'm Lindsey,' and took a step forward.

Child and dog stared equally impassively back at me. Both pairs of eyes were of the deepest brown, the dog's alight with intelligence, the child's shuttered and blank as pebbles. A cloud of soft black hair waved like smoke around her pointed little face. She wore jeans and a red jumper with a Paddington Bear design across the front.

Fixing a smile on my face, I bent down to their level and greatly daring, raised a tentative hand to the dog's head, hoping that the animal would not sense my nervousness.

To my untold relief, he began to thump his tail on the floor with great thwacks of apparent surrender, and allowed me to fondle his ears. Too much to hope that the child would be as friendly, though! Encouraged by the dog's acceptance of me, I went on stroking his smooth, bony head.

'I've come to stay here for a while. I've never been to Cornwall before and I'm hoping we can be friends. He seems to like me already, doesn't he?' I said with a smile.

Emma however, continued her unabashed stare without any reaction whatsoever, and my smile began to ache. The child's face was closed and I could read nothing from it. Then, with a deliberation which in a normally adjusted child would have been the height of rudeness, Emma turned her back, seized a book from the bed and stretched herself full length on her stomach as she began to idly flick through the pages.

Right, I thought, if that's the way of it, the next move shall come from you, young lady. Quietly I went back to my own room, leaving both doors slightly open. Then I began to unpack and put away my things, opening and closing doors and drawers noisily and humming a little tune to myself.

At the bottom of my case was a musical jewellery-box, which I had been given as a present on my tenth birthday. I couldn't bring myself to throw it out with the rest of the stuff when I moved, and now I was glad I had kept it.

It had always enchanted me as a child. When the lid was opened, a ballerina, wearing a pink and white spotted tutu, would dip and twirl in front of a tiny mirror to the tinkling music of the 'Blue Danube' waltz.

I placed the box on the dressing-table near the door and lifted the lid.

After a few moments I was aware of someone in the doorway behind me, but resisted the temptation to turn around. Carrying on tidying, I hummed along to the music. Then, as I turned to put some hankies in a drawer, I pretended surprise when I caught sight of Emma, who was gazing solemnly at the dainty dancer.

'Isn't she pretty? She dances when you raise the lid, you see?' I remarked offhandedly, and turned away, crossing the room to hang up a couple of shirts. 'You can play with it if you like.'

From the corner of my eye I watched the child silently put out a hand and finger the dancer's skirt. She closed the lid, then raised it again and when music filled the room, the ghost of a smile was hovering around the corners of her mouth. I could hardly resist smiling myself at the success of the simple ruse.

Our fragile moment of rapport was short-lived, however. Jane Harris suddenly appeared in the doorway and came bustling in.

'Bedtime, Emma,' she called peremptorily, and the child's face fell. 'You needn't go bothering Miss Lindsey tonight — she'll soon be seeing enough of you. You leave her settle in now.'

'But she's not bothering me,' I protested, furious as the housekeeper grasped the child by the hand. Emma went with her stoically, unresisting, with the shuttered look again upon her face.

'Goodnight, Emma. Come and play with the musical-box again tomorrow, won't you?' I called after her, but of course there was no response.

I could have berated the woman for her insensitivity, but it was too late, the damage was done. I silenced the music and went to have a shower.

Refreshed and revitalised, I opened the wardrobe and wondered what to wear. Something smart but not showy, and which didn't need ironing after being squashed in a suitcase.

I pulled out a black flared skirt and a shirt of multi-blues and greens. That should do. I studied my reflection in the full-length mirror inside the wardrobe door and decided that the figure staring back at me looked neat and professional — apart from her shock of rumpled black hair which was still standing damply on end. Green was always a safe bet, it flattered my eyes.

Ian had always jokingly called them, 'cat's eyes'. A spasm of pain crossed the shadowy face and I slammed the wardrobe door. Bury all those memories. This was a new life.

2

I paused at the foot of the stairs, one hand resting on the carved newel post, trying to remember whether Jane Harris had said the right or the left.

'In here, Lindsey.' Nicholas' voice came suddenly at my elbow. I was jumpy anyway and this shock did nothing to help.

'Oh, I didn't hear you coming,' I said, and managed a smile. I noticed he had smartened himself up and was now wearing a tie, along with neatly-pressed grey slacks and neck sweater of navy-blue.

'Come and meet the family,' he said. Pushing open the door, he stood politely aside for me to enter.

A babble of voices suddenly fell silent as I went in and immediately I found myself the focus of four pairs of curious eyes.

They were all seated around the pine dining table waiting for the meal to be served. A real fire burned in the old-fashioned grate and thick curtains of old rose colour were drawn tightly over the window. The room however, which should have been warm and cosy, was not. A thin draught was blowing under the door and nipping at my ankles and I wished I'd stayed in trousers.

'This is Lindsey, folks,' Nicholas announced and began the introductions. 'My mother, Jessica.' A pair of steely grey eyes looked me up and down, before the woman at the head of the table gave nod and a stiff smile along with her formal 'How do you do.'

'These are my brothers, Tim and John, and John's wife, Amy.'

'Hello everybody,' I said with a general friendly smile.

'Come and sit over here,' said Amy, 'I do hope we can be friends,' she added, with an earnest expression on her rather hard face. Flamboyantly dressed in a low-cut ruffled silk shirt and a dark green skirt, she wore dangling ear-rings which tinkled as she turned her head. This was John's wife, I reminded myself, as I took in the mass of flaming red hair.

'Lovely,' I murmured as I slid into the chair beside Amy. It would be nice to have a friend. But didn't she and John live in the annex? Why were they eating over here? To look me over? I just managed to smother a giggle as the penny dropped.

Nicholas passed me a bread roll and enquired, 'Have you settled in all right, Lindsey? I hope you like your room.'

'Oh very much so, thank you,' I replied, meaning it. 'It's a beautiful room, and the view is fantastic — it must be the best in the house.'

As I sipped my soup, deep inside my head a warning bell was faintly sounding. Hadn't the housekeeper said that it had been Rachel's room — Nick's dead wife? Had it been their room then? His and hers? And he could no longer bear to sleep there on his own?

Yet another voice broke in and the moment passed.

'So you're the new nanny,' remarked Tim, in a lazy drawl. He was leaning back in his chair, his hooded eyes insolently raking me up and down, and I disliked him instantly. 'You don't look much like one — ours used to wear a grey flannel suit that weighed a ton and a hat like an upturned chamberpot.' He sniggered.

'Shut up Tim,' Nicholas snapped and glowered at him.

'Actually,' I replied loftily, trying to stare him down, 'I'm a qualified educational psychologist. My last job was in a child guidance clinic in London.'

Jane Harris was removing the soup plates and bringing in roast beef as Tim's cynical voice went on, 'Personally, I can't imagine why you want to waste your money on a . . . what was the word — therapist?' looking not at

21

me, but at Nick. Lifting an eyebrow, he added, 'We all know that Emma's not going to get better. If she was it would have happened by now. Don't you agree, Mother?'

He turned to Jessica, who sat ramrod straight, her short wavy grey hair swept back from a bony, thin-lipped face. Her sharp eyes seemed to miss nothing of the verbal sparring between her sons, but her face softened as she shot Tim an indulgent look and replied, 'I do think so, Tim, dear, as you know. But,' she raised an eyebrow, 'my advice was completely disregarded.'

Her loaded fork paused in mid-air as she glared at Nicholas. 'Emma should have been sent to one of those excellent schools run by experts, right from the beginning. They would have known how to handle cases like hers.'

Jessica replaced the fork on her plate and clutched a bread roll so hard it crumbled to bits. 'I even offered to pay their exorbitant fees, but no . . . and now Nicholas, you see where your stubbornness has landed us. We've had to take a perfect stranger into our home, and probably all for nothing.' She returned to her meal and an uneasy silence fell.

I was mentally comparing the three Penwarne sons. Tim and John were light-haired like Nick but with blue eyes, not brown. Also, where Nick's features were handsomely chiselled, Tim had a weak mouth and chin and his eyes were heavy-lidded and secretive.

John, intent on his food, was more heavily-built, with the fresh pink cheeks of a countryman.

Amy's strident voice broke in. 'But I think Nick was absolutely right.' She looked defiantly at her mother-in-law, who ignored the remark.

'But then, you would,' retorted Tim, throwing her a sly look from under his heavy lids.

John's head jerked up and he looked speculatively from one to the other, before enquiring mildly, 'Do you mean right to keep Emma at home, or right to engage Lindsey, dear?'

'Oh, John, you haven't been listening again, have you?' snapped his wife. 'I don't know, darling,' she said with exasperation, 'sometimes I think you live in a world of your own.' She gave a shake of her head and stabbed her fork into a piece of beef.

John didn't speak again, but lowered his eyes to his plate. Well! I thought. He must be either a mouse or a perfect saint to let his wife put him down like that in front of everyone. But what an odd family this was. I scanned the faces round the table. All these adults still living at home with Mother! It's like something out of a gothic novel. No wonder they get on each other's nerves. What keeps them all here anyway?

I did a quick mental re-cap of what I had learned that evening. John and Amy first. An ill-match couple surely? She with her painted fingernails and he in country cords and an open-necked shirt. He tends the farm, so their

24

livelihood is here. Although Amy is hardly a typical farmer's wife.

Then Nick. He's forced to stay because of Emma. That leaves Tim. What about him? I was wondering where he fitted in when Nick spoke to me.

'Have you a family of your own, Lindsey?' he asked.

I swallowed hard. 'No, I haven't anyone at all — now,' I replied in a matter-of-fact voice, as Jane Harris brought in dessert. 'My mother died giving birth to me and my father was killed in a road accident soon afterwards.'

I had no intention of mentioning Ian. There was no guarantee I could control myself if I did. 'I was brought up by my grandmother, then I went to boarding school and on to university,' I added.

'That must have been tough.' Nick's eyes were gentle and sympathetic but I avoided his direct gaze and concentrated on the apple tart in front of me.

Topped with the local clotted cream, it was delicious and I said so, as much to change the subject as anything.

'Yes, Jane's a gem,' said Nick, 'I don't know what we'd do without her. When she serves the coffee, bring yours into the study. We still have a few things to sort out.' He excused himself and pushed back his chair. Soon the rest of the family began to drift away and I wandered after them into the lounge to fetch my coffee.

'I was surprised to be taken on without being interviewed by you,' I remarked to Nick as we sat with our coffee one each side of his desk again. 'You must have taken an awful chance on me!'

He chuckled and leaned back to stretch his legs. 'I've known David Leigh all my life. I trusted him to pick the right person. He's Emma's godfather, so he knew what he was doing.'

I saw again in my mind's eye the pleasant, fresh-faced solicitor who had conducted the business, and could

26

imagine him being a friend of Nick's. About the same age. From college days perhaps.

'Amy looked after Emma at first,' Nick remarked as he stirred his coffee. He balanced the cup and saucer on his lap as he gazed into the middle distance. 'She was doing my secretarial work — as she still does — but before she married John she used to come up from the village every day. When Rachel died and then we discovered Emma's trauma on top of it, I had no idea how we were going to cope. My mother didn't know what to do, she was all for sending Emma away for treatment, as you heard.'

He turned to face me and put the coffee cup on the desk. 'But I felt that would be all wrong, after the shock she'd already had. I couldn't leave my work, so when Amy offered, I jumped at it because Emma knew her slightly from seeing her around the house. But it didn't work out. Amy wasn't trained of course, only well-intentioned, and

Emma was too much for her. It was hopeless.'

He took out a packet of cigarettes and offered it to me, then lit one as I shook my head. He went on, 'I was pretty desperate, I can tell you Lindsey, when I put out that advertisement.'

'Well, I certainly hope I'll be able to help Emma. I don't expect it to be an easy ride, but I've got plenty of patience and I am used to children with emotional problems.'

'I wish you all the luck in the world,' Nick replied fervently. 'There's nothing I wouldn't give to see her laughing and shouting again like a normal child.'

He lowered his eyes and began to fiddle with a pen he'd picked up, clicking and unclicking it as he went on, 'Er — about my mother. You mustn't take it personally if she seems a little — well, unfriendly is too strong a word — aloof maybe.'

He tapped off some ash and said, 'She's not in the best of health for one thing. She has heart problems. Which is one reason why we employ a house-keeper. 'Oh — she loves Emma I know, but since Emma's become so withdrawn and silent, Jessica's been completely at a loss with her.'

He gave a rueful grin. 'Also I think it makes her feel frustrated to think she can't cope with the child, and that makes her angry. Then,' he replaced the pen and looked up at me, 'When she wanted me to send Emma to a special school, and I refused pointblank, we had a row. I was sure it would have been the worst possible thing to do. I still am,' his voice held a touch of defiance, as if challenging me to disagree.

I was wholeheartedly on his side and said so. 'Oh yes, it would. To uproot her after she'd already been through so much, would have done far more harm than good.'

'Great.' He looked relieved. 'I'm glad we agree.' He drained his cup and replaced it. 'It's a pity Emma never accepted Amy. She would have been better able to care for her needs than Mother, and I've never been too happy about giving Jane so much responsibility. Emma seemed to like Amy well enough before, and it would have been the ideal solution. I can't really understand it.'

'It was an instinctive reaction, I suppose,' I replied, sipping my own coffee more slowly. 'She may have felt Amy was trying to take her mother's place. Perhaps she resented her for being alive while Rachel wasn't.'

'Could be. Anyway, I'm so relieved that you're here now. Jane is still perfectly willing to look after Emma when you have time off, and to put her to bed at night, which will make you feel less of a 'nanny'. You were, after all, engaged for your professional qualities. But maybe you wouldn't mind getting her up in the morning, as her room is next to yours?'

He stubbed out his cigarette as I replied, 'Of course, I'll be glad to. I must get to know Emma on a personal level as well as a professional one and that means taking part in her daily life.'

I could hear a dog barking furiously somewhere outside and a male voice calling to it. 'Quiet Ben, down boy. Good dog.' The barking slowly subsided and I remarked into the silence which had fallen between us, 'Emma's very attached to the dog, isn't she? He was up in her room earlier.'

'They're almost inseparable, and I'm glad of it. It means she can go out and around on her own, and I always know she's safe. Ben's a very intelligent animal and would never let her come to any harm.'

'I was wary of him at first. I'm not used to dogs, but he seemed to accept me straight away, which was lucky.' I chuckled. 'It would have made my job even harder if he wouldn't let me come near Emma.'

'Dogs like Ben know instinctively whom they can trust.'

I finished my coffee as Nick straightened up in his chair and said in a business-like way, 'As to your position here, Lindsey, you'll live as one of the family of course, and you're free to take some time off when you feel like it. All I ask is that you let me or Jane Harris know when you're going out, and she'll keep an eye on Emma. Is the salary we arranged through the firm satisfactory?'

'Oh, yes, perfectly, thank you.' It was less than I'd been getting in London, but that was to be expected. And there would be far less to spend it on here.

'Good. That seems to be all for the time, I think. We'd better join the others. Or perhaps you'd rather go up to your own room?'

'Actually I would, if you don't mind. It's been quite a day.' I smiled. 'I could do with a quiet hour to settle in.' And to relax and sort out the jumble of impressions which my mind was wrestling with just then.

'Fine. I'll see you in the morning. Emma usually wakes between seven-thirty and eight. OK?'

We parted in the doorway and I

climbed the stairs again to my room. Through the window of the first landing I could see lights twinkling now about half a mile away. The village lay below the hill on which this house was perched, and was half-hidden in the valley bottom.

As I entered my room, my head full of other thoughts, I wasn't looking where I was treading and was brought up short by a crunch under my foot as I stepped on something. When I saw what it was, my hand flew to my mouth in dismay. It was the ballerina from the musical box. And the box too lay not far away, shattered to bits on the floor.

3

It was disappointing, but understandable. I was under no illusions as to the problems I was likely to face with Emma, and this was obviously the beginning of them.

I was picking up the pieces when Jane Harris appeared at the top of the stairs and stopped to watch. 'Oh, no! My dear life, what a thing for the child to do, after you was being so nice and all. Give she what for I would, in the morning. Can't leave she get away with that — mixed up or no'.'

The woman was red in the face with indignation, but I shook my head and said, 'No, I don't think scolding her would do a lot of good. This is Emma's reaction to my coming here. She probably feels threatened. I shan't make too much of it, that's what she wants me to do. She can't speak, so this is her way of telling me to go away.'

'Well, I wouldn't stand for it, if it was me.' She sniffed and bustled away to the walk-in linen cupboard nearby. I could see now what Nick meant when he'd mentioned giving 'too much responsibility'. It was another way of saying she hadn't the least idea of how to treat the little girl. A heart of gold no doubt, and full of good intentions, but Emma wasn't a normal child and shouldn't be punished for her actions as if she were.

I shut the door and took a look at the broken pieces in my hand. The damage wasn't actually as bad as I'd thought at first. The hinges of the box were broken and the mirror was cracked, but the thick pile of the carpet had protected the dancer when I had trodden on her and she could be glued on again. I could easily get new hinges and fix them on.

The mechanism still worked when I turned the key. So I did a temporary job with sticky tape and decided to put it back exactly where it had been and watch Emma's face when she saw it intact again in the morning.

Before I went to bed I crept quietly into the room next door to check on the child. She was sleeping peacefully in her small neat bed beneath a Peter Rabbit duvet, her cheek pillowed angelically on her hand like a stylised picture of a sleeping child. Dark lashes spread like fans against her delicate skin, and her cheeks were slightly flushed. She looked so normal and so loveable that it was hard to imagine her as she'd been earlier.

Exhausted as I was, I found it hard to get to sleep myself. So many pictures were dancing before my eyes it was like watching a video re-run, and my head was throbbing. Being in a strange bed didn't help either. Then just as I was beginning to doze off at last, I was suddenly jerked wide-awake by the lightening of the room. I hadn't bothered to draw the curtains and now a full bright moon was floating serenely by and having a good look in at me.

Furious, I threw back the covers and padded across the room to close the curtains. But the beauty of the night caught me by surprise and I sat down on the padded window-seat. It was so completely different from London nights that I had to convince myself I wasn't asleep and dreaming.

The moon hung over the almost invisible sea, which was pansy-dark and spangled with reflected light. The shadowy rise and fall of the land was made even more mysterious by the velvet night, and on the summit of a looming crag, a circle of huge standing stones was etched against the starry sky. They looked like hunched and brooding old crones, pointing granite fingers to the heavens.

The gleam of the moon threw their long shadows across the hill. In the utter absence of noise, the scene was awesome. Unnerving almost, to think of how many hundreds of years the stones had stood in that position, and how many times the moon had already circled their hoary shapes.

My eyes were aching now with the strain of peering into the distance, but I thought I saw a light flash suddenly near the stones, then vanish. It did not come again and I shivered, suddenly cold. I jumped back into bed and cocooned myself in the duvet.

I was already missing the central heating of my flat in Blackheath. Old houses like this were always draughty, and it was still only March. The bed had lost its warmth while I'd been star-gazing and I was another age before I actually dropped off to sleep.

When I awoke it was daylight and seven forty-five by my travelling clock. I must have slept like the dead when I slept at all, it only seemed five minutes ago that I was at the window.

My first thought was for Emma. I leapt out of bed, slipped across to the bathroom then hurriedly dressed in the first things I grabbed, an Aran sweater and jeans. I could hear movements next door, so I knocked gently and went in.

Emma was up and fully dressed, wearing the red jumper and jeans from the previous day. She was completely neat and tidy except for her hair, which was standing on end in a mass of tangled curls which she was trying to flatten with a hairbrush as I walked in.

'Oh, good girl, you're up already.' I smiled approvingly at her. 'Shall I help you with your hair?'

She let me take the brush from her and stood passively while I sorted out the tangles. I was as gentle as I could possibly be, but I must have hurt her as I tugged and pulled. She hardly flinched however and did not make a sound.

'This looks as if it hasn't had a good brushing for a long time,' I said. 'Who usually does it for you — Grandma?'

The eyes reflected in the mirror looked scornfully back at me. I had only said it to goad her into some sort of reaction. I tried again. 'Jane then, does she?' Emma stared back, obviously listening but expressionless.

'Right, that's better.' I noticed a piece of red ribbon lying on the dressing-table, the sort that would have come from a box of chocolates perhaps, or a florist. On impulse I reached for it and tied the dark hair up in a pony-tail. 'How about that, then? Do you like it? I think it looks good.' The eyes in the mirror widened fractionally, but I couldn't tell if she was pleased or not.

I put the hairbrush down. Emma was still regarding me in the mirror, her brows drawn down in a calculating stare. I had obviously set her wondering what was coming next. Good. 'Would you like to play with the musical box before we go down to breakfast?' I asked.

She hung her head at that and scuffed a toe in the carpet, but peeped slyly up at me out of the corner of her eye before she turned and ran out of the room. I followed and found her staring round-eyed at the box as she traced the crack in the glass with one finger. Then she poked at the sticky tape on the dancer's feet and where the hinges should have been.

'I'm afraid it had a bit of an accident. Someone must have knocked it over,' I remarked. There was a defiant look on her face now, as if she was waiting to be told-off.

I gave her a friendly smile. 'But it still works. Wind it up yourself and see.' I could have laughed out loud at the naked astonishment on the small face. She reached warily for the key and soon the tinkling of its music filled the room.

When it had run down, Emma lost interest, turned her back and scampered off downstairs. I caught up with her at the dining-room door. She slipped into her place at the table and began to sip milk from the glass ready for her there, and ignored the others.

Nick raised his head from the folded newspaper beside his plate. 'Hello sweetheart,' he said to his daughter across the table. She glanced briefly at him and helped herself to a slice of toast. Affection softened Nick's rugged features as he smiled at her. 'You're looking very pretty today. I like the new hairstyle.' He turned his head to include me in the smile, so I said a general 'Good morning,' and sat down. 'I wasn't sure how she usually wears it, but I thought this would keep it tidy.' I glanced at the shining dark curls and thought what a pretty child she could be. And felt a pang of sympathy for Nick as she totally ignored him.

Emma was carefully spreading her toast with butter and jam, without making a stain or dropping a crumb on the spotless tablecloth. She was precise and self-contained in her movements, and completely unchildlike.

Jessica had nodded curtly as I sat down, but said nothing and did not return my smile. Nick noticed and shrugged, shooting me a look that said, 'I told you so.' So this was what he'd meant. Oh, well, I could live with it.

To break the silence which seemed to have fallen, I said, 'I thought we might go out for a walk this morning, Emma and I. And Ben too, of course. They can show me around.' The child didn't move her head, but her eyes flicked up as she glanced at me from under lowered brows.

I smiled at her and turned to Nick saying, 'I'd like to have a closer look at that stone circle I can see from my window. What is it exactly?'

'Ah, those are the Dancing Maidens,' he replied, pushing aside his paper and empty plate.

I helped myself to cereal and he poured another cup of tea for himself and offered the pot to me. 'Thanks.' I pushed my cup towards him.

'You'd better ask Jane for the stories of all the standing stones and burrows you'll see around here.' He grinned at the housekeeper, who had just come in with more toast. 'As an archaeologist I'm only concerned with the scientific side of these things.'

'What are you working on at the moment?'

Jessica rose to her feet, excused herself and left the room. I had the impression that she was none too pleased to see Nick and me getting on together so easily. 'Yes, it's about the dig we're working on. It's very near here. As I was saying, I had to resign my teaching job in Birmingham when Rachel died.' He lowered his voice and nodded towards Emma's bent head, 'and come down here to live permanently.'

He stirred his tea reflectively. 'It was such an upheaval, you can't imagine. The only bit of luck I did have was to be taken on by the county archaeology unit. They were about to start excavating a site just half a mile away from here. It was perfect for me as I can live at home, and be with Emma.'

'Oh yes, I see.' I could only begin to understand the traumas that both he and Emma had been through. 'What are you excavating?' I shrugged.

'It's a Bronze Age settlement. We're coming to the end of the work actually.

Then what I'll do next I'm not quite sure. But at least, now that Emma has you to look after her, I shan't be so tied.' He nodded at the little girl, who was gazing out of the window and chewing toast. 'Would you like to come across and see the dig, Lindsey? You could walk over that way and I'll show you around.'

'Lovely, I'd like to.'

'Right, I'll see you outside in fifteen minutes,' he said, pushing back his chair.

Jane Harris had entered with a tray under her arm and was clearing the table. ''Tis all very well for Mr Nick to laugh,' she muttered darkly, a frown between her eyes, 'but I don't hold with it myself. Digging up old stuff like he do. It do only bring bad luck.'

'Bad luck? What do you mean, Jane?' I suppressed the urge to laugh out loud at the old-fashioned notion.

She stared at me with dark, deep-set eyes and I straightened my face. 'What I said. Three years ago the people came down here first, and started poking here and prying there. Digging and scraping. And what do happen? Mrs Rachel died and nothing haven't been right since.'

She rattled dishes on to the tray. 'Take that there child, poor little maid.' Her voice dropped to a whisper and she jerked her head in Emma's direction. 'Bad luck, see?' she repeated. 'Some things is best left buried and peaceful — don't no good come of disturbing the past.'

She shot me a look so intense that I actually felt the back of my neck prickle. 'I know you don't believe a word I do say, no more than Mr Nick do, but I've seen things over there after dark. Movements, and lights where no lights didn't ought to be. I know what I seen with my own eyes.'

I was speechless. She pointed a warning finger. 'And I aren't the only one, neither. You ask down the village — isn't many what will walk that hill by night. Haunted 'tis, see?'

She steadied the piled tray and left

the room without another word, leaving me goggling after her, with a creepy feeling right down my spine. For hadn't I too, seen a flicker of light up there? But this was the twenty-first century, for goodness' sake. I was a rational adult and there was no place in my life for ghosts and ghouls. I shook it all out of my system and went to fetch my coat.

I waited for Nick on the front steps, watching Emma as she threw sticks for the dog to fetch. I had decided I would play it cool initially with her, keep the relationship casual, and give her time to get to know me. Trying to get too close too soon could easily do more harm than good.

I shifted my gaze to the vast and empty landscape of boulder-strewn crags and wild, windswept moorland. The boulders tumbled to a sea the colour of slate, which reflected the leaden sky.

'Right, are we ready?' Nick's breezy voice made me jump as he appeared round the corner of the house. 'Emma!' he called, 'come this way.' The dog came lolloping up to him with the child trailing after it.

Nick closed the gate and I smiled as I read the name painted on it. Hawk Farm.

We fell into step then, following the rising ground. The track ran alongside a dry-stone wall and over a granite stile leading to the open moor. Here were the sheep I had seen in the distance, together with their lambs.

'Is this your family's flock?' I asked. Nick was holding out a hand to Emma as she clambered over the stile.

'That's right. John is probably some-where around. He keeps a close eye on them in the lambing season. Emma — keep hold of Ben until we're past the sheep. Good girl.'

We were getting nearer to the Dancing Maidens now. The stone circle towered above our heads, looming through the mist which still clung to the summit of the hill. 'You were going to tell me about the stones, Nick.' I grinned and added, 'from a strictly scientific viewpoint, of course.'

Nick threw back his head and laughed. Again I thought what an attractive man he was when he relaxed. But he had had little enough to laugh about in recent times of course. It took years off his face and right now he looked more like my own age of twenty-five.

'Well,' he replied, 'nobody, scientific or not, really knows why these great things were erected. They probably had several uses. One school of thought maintains they were used by primitive astronomers because they're aligned to positions of the sun and moon at significant times of the year.'

'What significant times?'

'Oh, the ancient Celtic festivals. I can't remember them all, but I've got plenty of books about it if you want to read it up.'

'Right, I might do that.' I wouldn't have given the subject passing interest before, but faced with such impressive remains, it did make me wonder about the people who had lived here once.

We stopped to let Emma catch up. Nick had planted one foot on a rock and was leaning on his knee, looking up at the stones. He was wearing hefty walking boots with a great many lace-holes, and thick woollen socks into which his cord trousers were tucked.

'Then again,' said Nick, 'some people think that the various standing stones could have been used as direction-finders by travellers. Many of them are visible one from the other, and would have helped people to cross the countryside using them as sighting-lines.'

'I can imagine that.' It seemed a sensible idea.

'Or they could have equally well been used for general meeting-places. Or religious ceremonies — you get the ley-line hunters and searchers into ancient mysteries, who swear that underground sources of energy run between them. The speculation is endless!'

'I had a strange conversation with Jane this morning,' I told him. 'She thinks that disturbing relics of the past like you do, brings bad luck.' My eyes met Nick's and he quirked an eyebrow.

'Jane is a kind and good-hearted woman,' he said, 'and an excellent housekeeper, but superstitious. Her family has lived here for generations and she's been brought up on all the old legends. Like the Dancing Maidens being young women turned to stone for dancing on a Sunday. Like the tales of mermaids, pixies and giants, which the tourist industry thrives on.' He pulled a wry face. 'Jane finds it hard to separate fact from fancy. So forget what she told you.'

'She said the hill is haunted.'

'Yes. She would,' he said tartly, then straightened up. 'Let's just say that my work is an analysis of the past which will benefit historians of the future. OK?'

'OK.' I dropped the subject and we walked on.

'Oh, that must be the site, is it?' I said as we came to the top of a rise and I could see activity on the opposite slope.

'Yes, we're nearly there. The hut circles were noticed from the air years ago. It wasn't until recently though that we could get the money to excavate. Do you know, we used to come up here and play among these mounds, my brothers and I. But I never thought then that I should be the one to uncover them!' Nick's face was alight with enthusiasm and I caught a fleeting glimpse of the schoolboy that was still there beneath the surface.

4

Nick gave me a tour of the half-excavated walls of the site, while Emma wandered off with the dog. Then conscious that I was keeping him from his work, I thanked him and detached myself and went to find her.

'Emma!' I called to the distant figure perched high up on a grassy bank, 'we're going back now.' She jumped down on to the path and came towards me. When she had caught me up, I said, 'Your daddy's busy, so you'll have to show me the way home and make sure I don't get lost on the way.' I smiled down at her and held out a hand, which she ignored, and with the dog trotting beside us, we set off together.

I made an effort to chat to her in a perfectly normal way as she walked, despite it being a one-sided conversation. I was convinced the child was listening and understanding, even though she didn't reply.

'I used to live in a big, noisy city,' I was saying, 'it's a change for me to be out in the countryside like this.' We were crossing a patch of springy turf starred with tiny, brilliantly blue flowers. 'Aren't these pretty?' I said, as I bent to pick one. 'I wonder what they're called.'

As I straightened up I could see John Penwarne striding down one of the fields to my right. He waved a hand and I noticed that he was carrying a lamb tucked under his other arm. As he came nearer he called, 'Emma — come and see what I've got.' Down on one knee at child-height he said, 'This is a sick little lamb. We're going to have to look after it indoors. Do you want to help?'

He spoke to her quite normally, just as I'd been doing and I warmed to him. He winked at me as Emma put out a hand and touched the lamb's woolly coat. I smiled back. He seemed to have a natural way with Emma, perhaps stemming from his closeness to animals. Used to dealing with the weak and helpless, a small child was not far removed from a wild creature in need of comfort.

It might do Emma some good to have the dependent animal to care for. 'I've never seen a lamb quite so small,' I said to him. 'But then I'm a city girl.'

'You'll find life very different here,' John said with his slow smile. He began to stroll along beside us. 'Do you think you'll like it, so far away from all you've been used to?'

I nodded. 'It's bound to take a while, but yes, I think I shall.' I was trying to convince myself, as much as John. For what alternative was there? It came again, that frightening feeling of utter rootlessness. Here I was, a stranger in a houseful of strangers. The paid employee, not quite a member of the family, always on the outside looking in. With no-one to call my own but my aged grandmother who had been only too glad to get me off her hands once I grew up. I took a deep breath of the crisp air. 'Especially if I can solve Emma's problems.'

'Poor little one. She's had a rough time,' John remarked, watching Emma running on ahead with the dog bounding at her heels.

'I'd like to know some more about your family,' I said, as I twirled the stem of the flower I had picked. 'I've only had the sketchiest impression of you all so far.

'By the way,' I showed him the flower, 'do you know what this is? We walked through a great patch of them back there. It's a beautiful shade of blue.'

John glanced at it. 'That's called squill. Vernal squill. You see it everywhere at this time of year. The turf is full of tiny flowers if you look closely, but most people don't see what they're treading on.' He grinned at me. 'Perhaps you have the makings of a country woman after all.'

'I did live in the country when I was

a small child. That was in Wiltshire, before I went away to school. The countryside is much softer and greener there.' I glanced around at the primitive, rock-strewn land of this outpost of England, exposed to the four winds and patchily covered with thin soil. I tasted its salt-laden air with my tongue and thought of the gentle undulating chalk downs of my childhood. Yes, the two couldn't be more different.

'I'm sure it is.'

John's eyes twinkled as he smiled and suddenly the image of Nick's laughing face overlaid that of his brother. But strictly speaking they weren't really alike. 'The family, did you say?' he looked blank.

'Yes. How long have you all lived here, John?'

'Well, the farm was originally my grandfather's — my mother's father, that is. His name was Chinn. He made a lot of money in mining shares. This used to be a great tin and copper-mining district. Botallack, Levant,

Geevor, they were all big names in their hey-day.' He pointed towards the sea. 'You can see some of the old workings from here. Look, those buildings half-way down the cliff.'

Perched precariously on a ledge leaning right out over the sea I could see the distinctive tall chimney-stacks and roofless engine-houses which were such a common sight in Cornwall.

John stopped to let me climb a stile and hitched the lamb carefully over his shoulder. This freed a hand to grasp the top step and he followed me over. 'Grandfather Chinn bought property, including Hawk Farm, which was in a dilapidated state then, and turned it into a small but prosperous farm. He gave it to my parents as a wedding present.'

'Where did your grandparents live then?'

'They had a big house on the outskirts of the village. As I said, they were well-off. They were pillars of the Methodist chapel too, and very well thought of in local society. Very respectable people.' He pulled a face.

'And your father?' I prompted. I needed to know the whole background from scratch if I was going to live with these people and get to know what made them tick. My trained and analytical mind wouldn't be satisfied with less.

John quirked an eyebrow, but continued to answer my questions without comment. 'My father came from a working-class background. Much lower down the social scale than the Chinns, do you know what I mean?' He looked at me as he changed shoulders with the lamb. I nodded. I knew enough about village life to imagine the unspoken nuances of behaviour, of which 'marrying beneath her' would have been one. 'Marcus was my mother's childhood sweetheart. He was a handsome man and could charm the birds from the trees if he tried,' John went on.

'Marcus was the eldest of seven children. His father was a miner.

Marcus was sent out to work at twelve to help keep the family. The sad part about it was, he was a clever man and would have dearly loved to study and make something of himself. He had a scientific mind. Always had his nose in a book — that's what I remember most about him. All those great volumes of astronomy and physics that are in Nick's study — they were all his.'

'Oh, poor Marcus,' I said with sympathy, 'did it make him bitter to be frustrated like that?'

'Huh, it made him absent-minded, I know that much,' said John with feeling. His expression was hard. 'He neglected the farm, it all went downhill while he was star-gazing.' John shrugged and the lamb bleated weakly in protest at the jolt. John soothed it with a large and gentle hand and murmured under his breath.

'The first few years were all right apparently. Tim and Nick were born into a life of luxury compared with what came afterwards. They even had a nanny. I can't remember that of course. I'm six years younger than Tim. Know I was set to work as soon as I could lift a bucket.'

'And the others as well, I suppose?' I was fishing. 'What does Tim do for a living?'

John snorted. 'Tim? He's never done a hard day's work in his life. He's an artist, you see.' He pulled a face. 'Nick never did a lot on the farm either. They were both clever at school, you see. I wasn't.' He glowered.

The psychologist in me was wondering about John. The third son, coming after two brighter brothers. Maybe his quiet manner concealed all sorts of private hang-ups.

'Now, as you can see, we've a few sheep left, but precious little else.' He waved an expressive hand. 'Things were very hard for Mother when we were growing up.'

'What actually happened to your father, then?'

'He — um — left us. After I was

born.' John's mouth clamped shut and the muscles of his jaw tightened. He turned away to whistle, unnecessarily, to the dog. Obviously he wasn't going to expand on that subject. 'Yes,' he went on, 'Mother had a lot of disappointments in her life. One of them was me.'

I stared at him and he shrugged. 'She'd wanted a daughter, not a third son.' He turned away to whistle up the dog. 'The long struggle made her very bitter towards Marcus. So much so that he couldn't take any more and he left. I believe he turned to someone else for comfort,' he added abruptly and changed the subject.

His eyes on the small figure of his niece who was throwing a stick for the dog, John remarked, 'I'm glad Nick stood up to Mother and didn't send Emma away. That child was bright as a button before Rachel died, and I'm certain that little girl's still in there somewhere if we could only reach her.' He sighed and rasped a hand over his jaw.

We were approaching the house now. 'Come on, Emma,' John called to his niece, 'let's find a box for our lamb.' The child trailed after him to an outhouse and they returned with a strong cardboard carton.

'We'll put this in front of the Aga,' he said as we went in. 'It'll be nice and warm there.'

I was so intent on watching them that I jumped in surprise when the door suddenly flew open and Amy burst into the room.

'Oh, there you are,' she said to her husband, completely ignoring both Emma and me. 'What on earth are you doing? It's way past lunchtime. For goodness' sake John, you could show a bit more consideration when I've got a meal on the table.'

She shrugged and held her palms upwards as she caught my eye. She fixed a smile on her face and said with false brightness, 'Men! They're all the same, aren't they?'

I said nothing. John replied patiently,

'Sorry, darling, just coming.' He straightened up and followed his wife out.

I was still goggling after them as Tim sauntered in through the open door and obviously noticed the amazement on my face. 'You're surprised at the way she speaks to him?' he observed.

'You heard? Yes, I am.'

'It's quite usual,' Tim said languidly. 'My brother's so cool and laid back he lets Amy walk all over him. He's never got over his surprise that she married him at all. He's besotted with her.'

'I didn't get the impression that it's mutual.' I raised an enquiring eyebrow.

'Oh, no it's not. Amy married John on the rebound. As second best, because she couldn't have the other Penwarne that she wanted.'

'Really? Who was that?'

'Nick.'

'Nick?' I heard my voice rise an octave.

'Uh-huh.' A smile lifted the corners of Tim's thin-lipped mouth. He had perched himself on a corner of the kitchen table, impeccably dressed in expensive and perfectly-fitting beige slacks and a sweater of moss-green lambswool. He folded his arms and surveyed my reaction with interest.

'She's been after Nick ever since they were at school. Mother encouraged her as well, but Nick just wasn't interested. Then when Rachel died, Amy saw it as her chance, and stepped in. But Emma wasn't having any of it, and Amy was forced out pretty sharply. Soon after that she married John — just to stay near her idol, I'd say.'

He slowly uncurled himself and slid off the table. He raised his eyebrows and strolled over to the fridge. He helped himself to sliced ham and began to butter a roll.

'Lunch in this place is a help-yourself arrangement,' he remarked. 'Has anyone told you? Jane loads the fridge and the cupboards and we come and go as we like.'

He piled a plate and left the room. I

stared at his retreating back. He was heading for the low building across the courtyard, next to the annex where John and Amy lived.

Nick met him outside and I heard him say, 'Lunchtime, is it? You're eating in the studio, obviously. Have you told Lindsey that we help ourselves to what we want?'

'I have,' replied his brother and glanced back at me over his shoulder. Annoyed to be caught listening, I stepped back. Tim Penwarne had a knack of catching me wrong-footed.

Nick leapt up the steps and entered the kitchen. 'Good grief, what's that?' he exclaimed, catching sight of Emma and the lamb.

'It's a sick lamb. John gave it to Emma to look after. She's doing a good job, isn't she?'

They stood for a moment side by side as Nick added, 'We'll have to think of a name for this little chap, won't we?' He chuckled and laid a hand on the child's shoulder. 'Emma had a little lamb,' he recited, 'it's fleece was white as snow . . . '

Then pity for Nick surged through me as Emma purposefully removed herself from his side and crossed the room without the slightest acknow-ledgement of her father. Nick's face fell, but he rubbed his hands briskly together and asked, 'Have you two had your lunch?'

I shook my head. 'No, not yet.'

'Well, let's see what Jane's left for us, shall we Emma?' He addressed the back of his daughter's head as she knelt in a chair and gazed out of the window.

I helped him put out food and plates and in a few minutes the three of us were sitting round the table with our snacks.

'Tim's an artist then is he? John was telling me.' So that's where he spends his time, I thought, as I forked salad on to my plate.

'Yes. He's quite talented, but I'm afraid he only works when he feels like it,' Nick replied tartly as he reached for the butter. 'My brother likes the easy life. I think he must take after our father. And as long as Mother keeps giving him an allowance,' he said tight-lipped, 'he's got no incentive to get a proper job.' Nick stabbed a piece of ham and slapped mustard on to it.

So Jessica gives Tim money, while Nick must have worked very hard to get where he is. Tricky. But Jessica had also offered to pay for Emma's treatment if she went away. So? For all I knew, she could even be paying my own salary. Unlikely, but possible.

Nick reached for a tomato and sliced it, placing some of the pieces on Emma's plate beside her sandwiches. She accepted them passively and picked up a fork.

'After we left school I went up to Birmingham and graduated, then took up lecturing. Tim won a scholarship to the Art School and stayed on in Penzance, but he dropped out halfway through, against everyone's advice.'

'Dropped out? Why was that?' I rose

to put the kettle on for coffee.

'Oh, he said he wanted to do his own thing.' Nick's expression was a mixture of amusement and distaste.

'So what did he do then?'

Nick reached for another roll and glowered. 'Oh, Mother fell for it and set him up in the studio here, and here he's been ever since. She's convinced he's a great artist in the making, whose talent must be nurtured. Plus, she likes having him around. She doesn't drive, and neither does John — only the tractor — so Tim made himself useful there while I was living away.'

He pushed a bowl of apples and bananas across the table. 'Fruit?' he offered, as I sat down with my mug of coffee.

'No thanks,' I said, but Emma helped herself to an apple and left the table with it, heading out of doors to play.

I watched her go and turned to Nick as a thought occurred to me. 'I haven't seen any pictures of Rachel around the house, and nobody seems to mention her much. Do you ever talk to Emma about her, or look at old photos together?'

Nick looked surprised. 'Well, no, of course not. It would only upset her even more, wouldn't it?'

'I don't think so,' I replied, absently stirring my coffee. 'When I was training and the subject of bereavement came up, we were told that everyone should be given the chance to express their grief. To weep, shout, throw things, whatever it took to get it out of their system. Then by doing that, one comes to terms with it and learns eventually to accept the loss.'

Nick looked dubious, but his eyes never left my face as I plunged on. 'You mustn't mind me saying this, but it seems to me that you've all naturally tried to shield Emma from further hurt and she hasn't had that chance.'

His expression darkened to a frown and I said hastily, 'Oh, I know you've showered her with presents, but when you think about it, there's actually no-one she can relate to on a one-to-one basis any more. And I think she's probably feeling her loss more than ever as time goes on.'

'But — ' Nick broke in, running his fingers through his hair in a gesture of bewilderment.

I shook my head and pleaded, 'Don't think I'm criticising you in any way, please. No-one can replace that special mother-child bond. I'm just suggesting that Emma's probably feeling lost and terribly lonely. Nobody understands her feelings and she of course, can't tell us.' I understood those feelings more than most. I could remember what it felt like to be a misunderstood and lonely little girl. And now a lonely adult too . . .

I pushed aside my empty plate and rested my folded arms on the table. 'She's too self-controlled for a six-year-old, Nick,' I said, willing him to share my conviction. 'My theory is that she's got all that shock and rage and pain at losing her mother so suddenly, still bottled up inside her. I know she appears good and well-behaved, but underneath I'm sure she's one insecure and frightened little girl. And that's what's showing up in her loss of speech. It's a kind of plea for help. Do you understand?'

Nick had ceased to eat and had been drumming his fingers on the table as he listened. At last he replied, 'Phew, I've never thought about it like that before. I give Emma as much of my time as I can, but with my work . . . '

'I know you do. As I said, I'm not criticising you in any way.'

'I don't know why nobody told me all this before. After all the specialists we went to . . . '

'Perhaps it wasn't so obvious then. And were they speech therapists?'

'Mainly, yes.'

'Then they weren't really on the right track. I'm sure Emma's condition is emotional rather than physical.' I glanced out of the window. Emma was kicking a football around the yard.

'It fits,' Nick said briefly. 'I've a

feeling you've come just in time, Lindsey.'

'Well, I think I understand the problem,' I said with a smile, 'whether I can solve it is another thing.' A silence fell as we each became lost in our thoughts.

'Nick,' I said eventually, 'would you mind if I talk to Emma about her mother? And if I ask you to do so as well? If it isn't too painful for you to go over old times with her.'

'Mm, yes, of course I will if you think it would help.' Nick nodded agreement and raised his glass to drain it.

'Perhaps you would let me have some photos too, so I can see what Rachel looked like. I might go over the happy times with Emma as part of the therapy. I can't be sure it will do any good, but ... ' I shrugged my shoulders.

'But we can try. Of course, Lindsey, do anything you like. I'll look out the photo albums. Mother'll know where they are. I haven't looked at photos since . . . but I'll let you have them as soon as I can.' He glanced at his watch and his eyes widened. 'Good grief, is that the time? I must get back to the site.'

He rose and pushed back his chair. 'Thanks, Lindsey,' he said and obviously meant it, 'you've made me feel more optimistic than I have for months.'

'Don't expect any instant results,' I warned him. 'It's bound to be a long and gradual process. You do realise that?' I was anxious that he would be too impatient to get disappointed.

'Of course I do.' He grinned, and something like hope or maybe relief, sparkled in his eyes. 'Sorry, must go. See you later.'

I sat on, my cooling cup of coffee forgotten, watching his long-legged figure stride away over the hill. It grew smaller as distance swallowed him up, until he was over the ridge and out of sight.

Having spent the rest of the day

indoors, by evening I could feel the beginnings of a headache behind my eyes, so after Emma had gone to bed I left the house to go for a stroll up the hill behind it.

The air was pleasantly cool on my hot forehead and the peaceful out-of-doors was soothing, I was jerked out of my own thoughts however, by the sound of a footfall coming up the slope behind me. I turned and was surprised to see Nick rapidly catching me up, his long loping stride making short work of the incline.

'Hi, Lindsey, we both seem to have had the same idea. I quite often come up here for a spot of fresh air in the evenings. Mind if I join you?'

'Of course not,' I replied. What else could I have said? But I'd actually been enjoying the solitude.

We'd reached the top of the rise and I paused for breath. The sky was darkening rapidly as the twilight thickened, Hawk Farm had vanished into the shadows and out at sea a scatter of lights winked over the almost invisible water. 'Fishermen setting their crab and lobster pots,' remarked Nick, following my gaze. 'They've come out from Sennen or Newlyn.'

'How quiet it is,' I said softly. I'd opened my mouth to say something else, when suddenly a piece of the night sky dived out of nowhere and swooped low, just skimming my head. I shrieked, shattering the silence around us, and ducked. I clapped both hands over my head and turned to Nick in an instinctive reaction, burying my face against his chest. He chuckled and patted my shoulder consolingly. 'Don't be afraid. It's only a bat.'

'A bat? Ugh!' I shuddered.

'They're perfectly harmless you know,' he said gently. I lifted my head and met his eyes, which were looking down at me, full of concern. I was feeling slightly foolish now at over-reacting.

I was also angry with myself for subconsciously enjoying the feel of his reassuring arms. It had been a long time since I'd been physically close to another person, and everything in me cried out for comfort.

I was always aware to a greater or lesser degree of the pit of pain inside me, lurking to catch me at an unguarded moment and now it stabbed through me with an almost physical punch. I dragged myself reluctantly away from the warm circle of Nick's arms and struggled to clamp the lid on it.

I pulled myself together. 'I must go back for my jacket,' I said, adding with perfect truth, 'it's colder than I thought.' I'd come out of the house without thinking, and my arms were bare.

'You're right,' Nick agreed and waved a hand as I turned back towards Hawk Farm and he carried on up the hill. By the time I had emerged from the house for a second attempt, he was nowhere to be seen and I had all the solitude that I wanted.

Once on the brow of the hill I stayed on for a while, gazing out to sea and then craning my neck upward as I tried to identify the few stars that I knew. I was standing in the shadow of one of the Dancing Maidens at the time and imagined I was the only person on the hill. So when I caught sight of a flicker of movement on the path just below me, I started with surprise.

I almost called out assuming it was Nick, but for some reason I stopped myself just in time. I'd feel a fool if it wasn't him.

I fixed my eyes on the spot where the path would bring the walker up to the stones, and looked over my shoulder. Then I had the fright of my life.

It had become much darker now as the evening advanced, and I was straining my eyes to peer through the shadows. But as I saw the black-clad, hooded figure which was advancing towards the stones, gliding soundlessly towards me, I had to clap my hands over my mouth to stifle a scream of pure, primeval terror. The ghost! I was alone on the carn with the apparition that was supposed to haunt it, and it was coming straight for me.

This was what Jane Harris had meant. This was why no-one would come this way by night. I shrank back against the tall stone where I was standing, and made myself as small and inconspicuous as possible.

He — it — came nearer, its face obscured by the hood as it passed right by my hiding-place. I had turned my face to the stone, afraid its glimmering paleness would give me away. My hands were still clamped to my mouth, the hairs on the back of my neck prickled, and I was shaking with terror.

I don't know how long I stood there frozen to the spot, but when I at last summoned up enough courage to turn my head the slightest bit, I could sense that the danger had passed. I peered all round the stone, and greatly daring, lifted my head to see the apparition descending the slope away from me.

My heart turned over with a lurch as I recognised that tall figure. The long, loping stride, the set of the shoulders, the way he walked. And, when drifting on the calm and peaceful evening air came a wholly recognisable and utterly normal scent of cigarettes. That spectre had been Nicholas Penwarne, no less. Suddenly I was furious. Furious at having been taken for a ride. Furious with myself to think how scared I'd been. Furious that he should be playing some kind of practical joke and even more furious that I had fallen for it.

Fury made me heedless of the very real risk of injury as I tore down the hillside after him. But I had already wasted too much time. The further down the hill I went the darker it became. Shadows of humps and bumps in the landscape loomed to disorientate me and roots and rocks under my feet conspired to trip me up.

At last was forced to slow down for safety's sake and to acknowledge the fact that I'd lost him. I looked up and around to see where I was — I'd been so intent on watching where I put my feet, that I'd lost all sense of direction, but I found I was quite close to Hawk Farm. I made a mental note of my bearings, for I hadn't finished with this business yet. I wanted to find out why my employer was playing stupid tricks up here and scaring half the village witless.

5

A couple of days later, I was sitting alone in the lounge after dinner, leafing through a women's magazine, when Jessica came in. Clad in a pink sweater and a skirt of grey and pink check, she was carrying several photograph albums as well as a handful of plastic bags holding loose prints.

'Nicholas told me that you wanted to see these,' she said without preamble, and dumped the whole lot down on to a small table beside me.

'Oh, yes I did, thanks.' I smiled at her and put aside the magazine. I was amazed to see her pull up a chair and settle down to show them to me.

'They're in chronological order except for the most recent ones,' she announced. 'The rest are still in those bags.'

She opened one of the albums and

placed it on my lap. 'These are the early ones — of my own children.'

I turned the pages and pretended interest. I hadn't the heart to tell her I was only really concerned with Nick's family. She was making an effort to be friendly, after all.

Jessica turned a page or two. 'This is Nick and Rachel's wedding,' she remarked. I sat up and took notice. Petite, her hair cascading in dark waves to her shoulders, Rachel smiled up at her new husband and clung lovingly to his arm. Nick looked down at her, his face tender, his free hand holding the grey topper which complemented his formal morning suit. They looked so happy I felt my throat tighten. To think that only five years later . . . But at least they'd had that five years together — five more than I'd done.

'And all the rest are here,' said Jessica briskly. 'The ones of Emma as a baby, with Nick and Rachel, which you particularly wanted, I believe.' She stood up and shrugged her shoulders. 'I hope you know what you're doing.'

'Yes,' I replied firmly, 'but this isn't just a job, you know. Of course I mean to do the best I can for Emma, but I really care about her too.'

Jessica sniffed. 'You'd better take these and I'll put the other albums away,' was all she said before turning on her heel and leaving the room.

Next day, a curtain of rain came sweeping in from the sea. It was a perfect opportunity to bring out the photos.

'Let's go up to your room and find something to do, shall we?' I said to Emma after breakfast. 'We certainly can't go outside today.'

I led the way upstairs while Emma trailed listlessly behind me.

'I've got a little job here that you can help me with,' I said to Emma as I brought out the box where I'd put all the appropriate photos. 'Your Grandma has given me all these photos to sort out, look. We're going to put them in this book. I'll need you to tell me where each one should go in its proper order, starting with the earliest. Let's sit at the table, shall we?'

I squashed myself into one of the child-size chairs which stood at a play-table in the bay window. Emma sat down opposite me and watched impassively as I tipped the photos out, deliberately leaving them face down.

Surprisingly, without being told, the child reached out a hand and began turning them over. Having gained her interest, I chattered away to her, making the most of it. 'Look, here's one of a little baby. That must have been you.' I smiled across at her, but Emma's eyes were unfathomable and she didn't return the smile.

'I think it would be a good idea to put them in order of age, so we could start with that one, shall we?' I placed the photo in one of the pockets of the first page. 'Now, can you find any more of you when you were very little?' I asked. Silence fell, but the child was gazing at the pictures, so I held my breath and didn't hurry her.

I could hardly believe it when she actually put out her hand and chose one. She stared at it for a long moment, until I said, 'That's a nice one. You in your pram with Mummy and Daddy taking you for a walk. Shall we put that next in the book?' Emma didn't react, so I leaned over and took it from her. 'Now which one, do you think?'

She made no further move, so I chose a picture of Rachel holding Emma aged about three. They were on a beach with the remains of a picnic nearby. Emma was wearing a mob-cap sun hat which framed her chubby face and she was clutching a bucket and spade. Rachel's sun-glasses were pushed up into her hair, which was blowing in strands across her face. Both of them were laughing into the camera at some unseen joke.

'You were having a good time there on the beach, weren't you?' I remarked matter-of-factly, 'with your mummy. What a pretty lady she was, wasn't she?'

I chose my words with care and watched. The little girl's eyes had widened. She was looking directly at me and seemed to be taking it all in.

I picked up another photo. This time Nick and Rachel were hand in hand with an older Emma. It must have been one of the last of them all together, and the dog, Ben, was in the background, so it must have been taken on a holiday visit.

'Oh, here you are again with Mummy — and Daddy too, this time. I wonder who took the photo. Perhaps it was Grandma, do you remember?' I tried. Emma was still looking and listening. I was almost sure she was on the verge of answering the question. Wishful thinking, perhaps.

Then to my amazement the child suddenly snatched the photo from me, slid off her chair and crossed the room to her Wendy house. She went inside and pulled across the curtain which served as a door.

I was thrilled to bits at having

brought about any reaction at all, and grinned to myself as I carried on filing away the photos. I hummed under my breath as I worked, and presently Emma reappeared, without the picture, and stalked across to the bathroom.

While she was out of the room, I streaked across to the Wendy house. Then my chin hit the floor — the photo had been torn to shreds and the pieces strewn all over the floor.

I hardly knew whether to be glad or sorry. Glad to have brought about a response, certainly, but what to make of it? Emma could be starting to release her inner tensions by rage — perhaps at her mother for deserting her. In which case this could be the beginning of a healing process. Or was it sheer destructiveness, and aimed at me? Her way of telling me to get lost and leave her alone? Perhaps she saw me as a threat to the defences she'd built, which were her security. Only time would tell.

★ ★ ★

That night I suffered the first nightmare I'd had since coming to Cornwall. I'd thought the bad dreams a thing of the past after all this time.

I hadn't been consciously thinking of Ian at all when I went to bed, my head had been full of other things entirely, but in my dream I was looking down at a sleeping figure I knew was him. As I watched, the figure raised its head to look at me and I was just about to see the face — Ian's beloved, laughing face — when it turned into a grinning skeleton and vanished.

I leapt out of bed in terror and caught sight of my ashen face in a mirror. My bottom lip was streaming with blood — I must have sunk my teeth into it during the nightmare. That was all. Calm down, I urged myself, it was only a bad dream, but the blood was still dripping down my nightshirt and I couldn't find a tissue. So, to the bathroom I thought. Wash it off.

I wriggled into a robe and stumbled across the room. Still struggling to shake off the aftermath of shock, I crossed the landing not really looking where I was going. And cannoned straight into a tall, looming figure who was standing outside the door. I opened my mouth to scream, but a hand fastened round my mouth and an arm like steel immobilised me as I kicked and squirmed in a fruitless attempt to free myself.

'Lindsey! Lindsey! What on earth is it?' A voice persistently calling my name penetrated my consciousness at the same time that I felt someone shaking my shoulder. The steel clamp was still over my mouth but it was Nick's voice I could hear. Nick!

I tried to pull myself together and control my hysteria. 'I'll take my hand off your mouth if you promise not to scream again,' he hissed in my ear. 'OK?'

I nodded and gasped for breath as, still with an arm around my shoulders, he hustled me towards the stairs. 'Downstairs, quickly, before we wake the household, then you can tell me all about it. Come on.'

His firm grip propelled me forward and I let my head lie against the comforting warmth of his body, which smelled of soap and toothpaste. Right now my need for simple human contact was so great that I couldn't care less about the proprieties. So I clung to the sleeve of his navy-blue bath-robe like a child to its comfort blanket, as he steered me into the kitchen, closed the door and snapped on the light.

He disentangled himself from my clutches and set me down in a chair beside the Aga as he reached for the kettle. Now I could see that his robe had been hastily tied, and that his hair was sticking up in little damp tufts.

Suddenly I was aware of appearances, I glanced down at myself. My own robe was open where I'd flung it on in a hurry, and the front of my nightshirt was covered with the blood which was still welling out of my bitten lip. I ran my tongue over it. It felt stiff and sore and I could taste the peculiar metallic flavour which blood has. I felt sick and my stomach heaved.

'Tea's on the way,' Nick announced, busy with mugs and spoons. I wrapped my arms around myself and hunched against the cushions, shaking still in every limb.

Nick set down a steaming mug on the floor by my side. He stayed on his knees as he said, 'Now, let's have a look at you,' and placed one finger under my chin. Gently he turned my face towards the light. 'Good grief, what have you done to yourself?' His eyes widened as they followed the trail of bloodstains down my front.

I tried a smile, but winced in pain instead. 'I had a nightmare,' I said, 'a bad one.' Talking was uncomfortable too, I had to use the side of my mouth. I must be looking as much of an idiot as I feel, was my immediate reaction. I picked up the mug and cupped my hands around its warmth. I wondered how I was going to be able to drink from it. 'Then I bit my lip and it's been bleeding all over me.'

'It still is,' Nick remarked. He grabbed a wad of tissues from a box on the window-sill. 'Here.'

'Thanks.' I released one hand from the mug and held the pad to my face. I looked longingly at the cooling tea.

'Drinking straws, that's what we need,' he said as if he'd been reading my mind. 'I wonder if Jane's got any.' He looked hopefully round the room as if trying to conjure some up.

'In the drawer of the dresser,' I replied with a flash of recall. 'I saw her give Emma one for her juice the other day.'

'Great. Yes, here we are,' Nick said, rummaging. 'Try that.'

'Mm, thanks.' I sucked gingerly at the straw. 'I do feel foolish, causing such an upset. I'm sorry I woke you, Nick.'

'I hadn't been to sleep. I'd been reading until quite late, then I went to have a shower. I was just coming out of the bathroom when you barged into me.'

I was clutching the mug tightly in case I spilled it, as my hands were still shaky, and he noticed. 'It must have been some nightmare,' he remarked. 'What was it about, can you remember?'

'Oh, yes.' I shuddered. 'I remember.'

I looked into the quizzical blue eyes looking at me with concern, and something turned over inside me. It was very snug and quiet in the kitchen. Thick curtains kept out the sound of the wind and sea. Nick had opened the fire door of the Aga, which was giving out a comforting ruby glow. We could have been the only two people on earth.

'It was about Ian,' I said, gazing into the fire.

'Ian?'

'He was my fiancé — a soldier. He was killed in Northern Ireland. A sniper's bullet . . . We were going to be married when he got back.'

To my undying shame I couldn't

prevent the tears from coming then. I set down the mug and fumbled with the wad of tissues in my hand. Nick, who had perched himself on a corner of the table, leaned across and placed a hand over mine, giving it a gentle squeeze. It felt like a red-hot branding iron to my frayed nerve-endings, and I gave an involuntary jump.

'Oh, Lindsey, I'm so sorry. That's a pretty feeble thing to say, I know, but it's all there is. Believe me, I know what it feels like,' he added quietly, his eyes holding mine.

I nodded, and as I gazed into Nick's face, the revelation hit me. How like Ian he was. Not in colouring — Ian had been dark, with curly hair — not exactly alike in anything I could put my finger on, but there was something, an expression, the lift of an eyebrow, the way his mouth turned up at the corners, which had been tugging at my subconscious for weeks.

That was why I felt drawn to this man, I thought dully. The man with hidden secrets who was no longer to be trusted. I felt my shoulders droop as I removed my eyes from his face and twisted the sodden tissues I was still holding.

'When Rachel died, I wanted to die too,' Nick said painfully. 'Although I knew it was inevitable the shock when it happened was still as great. As you know. I couldn't take in the fact that she just — wasn't there any more.' He removed his hand to run agitated fingers through his already spiky mop of hair, then fell silent for a few moments, staring into the fire.

'How's our mouth now, by the way?' he asked abruptly, changing the subject.

'Not as bad as it was. The tea helped, I think. It's stopped bleeding anyway.'

'I've been thinking,' he went on, 'about what you said to me the other day about Emma. How everyone has to purge themselves of grief when something like this happens. By weeping, or screaming, or throwing things. Do you remember? And I realised that was what

I never did at the time.' He looked me squarely in the eye and added, 'And I guess you haven't done, either. Am I right?'

Caught unawares, I flinched from his probing look. But he was right. 'Yes, actually,' I said and smiled tentatively with my swollen lips. 'I was so intent on putting on a brave front and not giving myself time to brood, that I didn't practise what I preach at all.'

'Me, too. I've been forcing myself to put on the stiff upper lip act for the last two years, for Emma's sake.' He leaned across and patted my hand again. 'I owe you a great deal, Lindsey,' he said.

This time I steeled myself to feel nothing and almost succeeded until his eyes met mine and I could see the tenderness in them. For a long moment, time seemed to stand still and we were wrapped around with warmth, not all of it from the glowing fire. Then something caught my eye. Movement. I had seen a flicker of movement behind the glass of the outside door.

The door was half-glazed, the top half having a clear panel over which hung a net curtain. Hazily through the net I'd seen the pale shape of a face peering in at us. I felt myself stiffen and draw in a quick breath, then Nick whirled round, following my eyes. 'What is it?' he said in alarm.

'There's someone there — outside, looking in. I saw a face through the glass,' I stammered. 'But,' I added lamely, 'it's gone now.'

Nick jumped up and made for the door, grabbing a torch from the window-sill as he went. He was in the yard in seconds, snapping on the outside light and swinging the powerful torch in all directions. Its beams soon dispelled any lurking shadows, and he shook his head as I came to the doorway looking after him.

'No, there's nothing there now,' he said. He came back inside and bolted the door. 'Was it a man or a woman?'

'I don't know,' I lied, 'it was gone so suddenly.' But not before I'd identified the head of flaming hair which had shone red-gold in the light from the kitchen.

I sighed, suddenly overcome with weariness as I reminded myself again that the hand which had just been laid so comfortingly on my own was after all the hand of a man who walked the hill by night for his own obviously clandestine purposes, and I must never let myself forget it. Although he had sat there talking so convincingly of his grief, I couldn't afford to trust him.

I dragged myself to my feet. 'I must go back upstairs and wash,' I said woodenly. 'Thanks for the tea. Goodnight.' I turned on my heel and left, ignoring the surprise on Nick's face and the hurt look that lingered in his eyes.

Back in bed in a clean nightshirt, the effects of the nightmare now obliterated apart from my sore mouth, it was a long time before I slept.

6

I had an idea I wanted to put to Nick, so a few days afterwards, when I'd seen him go into the study one morning I knocked on the door and poked my head round it. I hadn't realised that Amy was there as well. She was just putting a sheet of paper into the typewriter and Nick was standing at the bookshelves with his back towards me.

'Sorry to bother you, Nick. Could I have a quick word if you're not too busy? Hello, Amy, I didn't know you were here.' She gave a faint smile which didn't reach her eyes, and began to type.

'Of course, Lindsey, come in.'

'I won't interrupt your work for more than a minute — it's just that I thought of something that would be the ideal thing for Emma.'

'Oh, yes? What's that?' Nick perched

on a corner of the desk, looking intrigued.

'Well, when I was in London I went into one of these Young Learner Centres — they're a kind of educational toy shop — to buy a present for a friend's child. And I saw one of these small computers there. The children were queuing up to play on it, it was that popular, and I watched them.'

'Oh? A computer?' Nick raised his eyebrows.

'Yes, but nothing like you mean by the word. This is an educational aid. It had different programmes for various ages, on cards, each with a lesson on it. It seemed to me exactly the right thing for Emma. I could teach her on it, Nick.' I leaned forward and drummed my fingers on the desk, willing him to understand. 'She could press buttons for the answers and we could really communicate — without her having to speak.' I had to pause for breath and laughed. 'Sorry, I'm getting carried away here!'

Nick smiled back. 'I think it's a great idea,' he said.

'I'm hoping it will help to bring her out of her shell,' I replied. 'Can we get one of these locally, do you think?'

'If there's a good toy shop, of course we can. Shall I look in the phone book?'

'Sure. Could you pass the phone book, Amy, please?' he called over the clatter of the keys. She handed it to me with a 'tut' of annoyance and reached for the Tippex as if it was my fault she'd made a mistake.

I flicked through the pages. 'Yes, there's one in Truro.' I handed the book to Nick who read the address.

'Fine, I know where that is. I hope they've got one. I'll ring later and find out, then I'll let you know, OK?'

★   ★   ★

When I realised how the time had flown since I had come to Hawk Farm, I told myself I really must go down the village

102

to call in at its only shop and buy some postcards to send to the friends I had promised to keep in touch with and had never done. Emma was happy to play in the garden so I strolled the pleasant half-mile down the high-banked narrow lane and reached the village via a granite stile.

As I entered the combined shop and Post Office the buzz of conversation suddenly ceased and all eyes turned to me in undisguised interest. I gave a vague and general smile directed at no-one in particular and crossed to a stand of postcards, full of alluring photos of sun-kissed beaches and azure seas. I chose a handful and approached the woman at the counter.

'You're up at Carn Wartha, aren't you, my handsome?' she said. 'Looking after that poor little maid, are you? She isn't no better yet, then? Can't speak nor nothing, can she?'

'Not yet,' I replied grimly, 'but we're working on it.'

'Bleak old place up there, isn't it?'

she went on as she put the cards into a paper bag. Slowly she folded over the top and leaned across the counter. Lowering her voice she added, 'You haven't seen nothing I suppose, have you?'

'Seen anything?' I repeated blankly, pretending ignorance in case I learned something, 'like what?'

'Oh nothing,' she said off-handedly as she handed over my change and my purchase.

I recalled what Jane Harris had said, ' . . . there isn't many what will walk that hill by night. Haunted 'tis . . . ' By my employer . . . ? Oh God, what had I got myself into? And a cold shiver feathered down my spine.

A few days later I was leaning over the gate watching Emma tossing a ball for Ben to fetch and watching the sinking sun turn the sea into a sheet of beaten copper, when John came up the lane and stopped beside me. After a few general remarks regarding the weather, I decided to quiz him about a chance remark that Jessica had let fall one day, and which had set me wondering ever since.

'John,' I said slowly, 'I've been meaning to ask someone about this. Perhaps you can tell me.'

He glanced back at me over his shoulder. 'Oh, what's that?'

'Your mother mentioned that Emma gave Amy a rough time just after Rachel died. When Amy started looking after her. Yet she seems such a docile child now. I was wondering what made her change.'

'Oh, well now,' John took in a deep breath and his eyes swept over the hills as he replied, 'let me think. You must understand that Nick and Rachel only used to come down here for holidays before she died. Although Emma knew Amy worked for Nick, she didn't know her well. It was Mother's idea that she should look after Emma, while Mother tried to persuade Nick to send her away.'

'So Amy was little more than a

stranger to Emma. You weren't married then?'

'Oh, no. We've only been married just over a year.' He paused and scratched his head in thought. 'As far as I can remember about Emma, I've heard Amy say that she used to wet the bed and had to be punished for that, and — '

'Punished?' I couldn't help breaking in, 'How?'

'Oh, I don't know now,' John replied impatiently. 'I think she started sleep-walking too, at about the same time. So she had to be locked in at night for her own safety.'

My jaw dropped. A four-year-old? I tried to hide my indignation.

'Amy did her best,' said John defensively.

'So Amy gave up shortly after?'

'Yes, and I don't blame her, after she tried so hard.' His eyes softened. 'She's one in a million, Amy is. I'm a lucky man to have a wife like her.'

I bit my lip and said nothing. Ben's

excited barking reminded me that the two were waiting for me. We were going for a walk. 'Thanks John, I'd better go, by the sound of it.' John waved a hand and vanished around the side of the house.

I took child and dog down the lane and across the main road to the broad sweep of open moor which stretched to the sea's edge. As we went I was thinking about what John had said. I watched the bobbing figures as Emma threw sticks for the dog to fetch, and scampered about among the heather and gorse. From where I stood there was nothing to distinguish her from any normal child. How much had Amy's insensitive treatment contributed to her present condition? I wanted a word or two with Amy.

After about half-an-hour the weather seemed to be changing. I squinted up at the sky as an unexpected clump of grey clouds came scudding in from the sea, and am ominous dampness of the air warned of a shower to come.

'Emma,' I called, 'time to go back.' I pointed skywards and she obediently slipped the lead on to the dog's collar and came to stand beside me, ready to cross the road.

I could hardly believe it when I felt a small warm hand slip into mine, and stay there. I gave it a gentle squeeze and walked on air all the way back. It was the first crack in the wall of total indifference which Emma had shown to me from the very beginning, and it convinced me that it was not after all, too late to get through to her.

I met Nick in the passage outside his study. From within came the clatter of the typewriter and I caught a glimpse of Amy's red head bent over the keys. I must have been smiling to myself, for he said, 'You're looking very happy today, Lindsey. How are things going?'

'They could be improving actually. I think Emma's beginning to accept me.' And I told him how she had voluntarily taken my hand. 'It may seem only a small thing, but I was quite excited.'

'Oh yes, that's wonderful! Perhaps it's a turning-point. Do you think so?'

His expression was so pathetically eager than I hastened to add, 'I shouldn't go as far as that, Nick — it's bound to be a very gradual process.'

'Of course. Anyway, I've got some good news too. I picked up Emma's computer today. It's in the study.'

'Oh, good. Now I can really set her to work.'

'I opened it up to have a look.' Nick was lifting a cardboard box from his desk and putting it on the floor. 'It's fascinating. I can see exactly what you mean, and I'm sure she'll love it. I'll just unplug it from the socket — there.'

'Thanks. I'll take it up with me now.'

Amy's voice broke in as I turned to leave. 'I must go and post these letters, Nick, if you want them to go tonight.'

'Right, thanks,' he replied and she followed me out of the door.

Here was the chance I'd been waiting for. As we walked down the passage together, I casually remarked, 'John was telling me earlier about the trouble you had with Emma, just after her mother died.'

Amy tossed her flaming head, setting her earrings tinkling. 'I should say so. She nearly drove me mad. What with tantrums, and sleep-walking — and wetting her bed every night. A big girl like that wetting the bed!'

'How did you cope with her?' I prodded.

'Oh, I used to put her in the cupboard under the stairs and shut the door on her — oh, only for a minute or two,' she added, and knew she'd seen my horrified face. 'Just long enough to teach her a lesson.'

We had come to the bottom of the stairs and paused as I was about to go up with the computer, when Nick came out of the study and caught us up.

'I tried so hard with her, didn't I, Nick?'

'Sorry, what was that?'

'I was telling Lindsey how had I tried to be a second mother to Emma. But

110

you know I did, don't you?' She was almost pleading.

I was looking at Amy as she raised her face to Nick. All her heart was in her eyes and the message was unmistakable. She does love him, I thought. Still. I looked at Nick. His expression was unchanged as he off-handedly replied. 'Ah, yes, that's right,' and walked on.

He's never loved her, I thought. Hmm. 'Only,' I went on, 'I've never known Emma do any of those things since I've been here.'

She shot me a venomous look. 'Since she's been left to run wild and do exactly as she chooses, it's not surprising. Anyway, I've got to get these in the post,' she snapped.

★   ★   ★

Next day after having spent time with Emma and her new 'toy', I was running downstairs feeling quite cheerful to think how well she had adapted to it — in fact I could hardly prise her away from the screen — when Nick came out of the study as I was passing. His head was half-buried in a sheaf of papers and he glanced up with a brief smile.

'Emma's spent most of the day playing with the computer,' I said.

'Oh fine, fine.' Nick's response was only lukewarm and not what I'd expected. I stared at him deflated, my smile slipping off my face in disappointment. His brown eyes were abstracted, and he was deep in his notes again.

He snapped suddenly out of his preoccupation as if he had just seen me properly. 'Sorry, Lindsey,' he apologised, 'but I'm in a bit of a state here at the moment.' He indicated the papers in his hand.

'Oh, in what way?'

'Well, Amy's mother's been taken ill and she's gone down to the village to look after her. I know it can't be helped,' he sighed, 'but it's an awful nuisance. She was going to type up this report for me and it has to go off today.' Then his face brightened as he looked at me. 'I don't suppose you can type, can you?' he said eagerly.

'Me? Oh, yes, as a matter of fact I can, but . . . '

A smile like sunshine spread across his face. 'Oh, would you, Lindsey, please?'

'Well — I suppose so. But someone will have to keep an eye on Emma. Mind you,' I made a point of saying, 'she's so immersed in her computer at the moment that she won't be much trouble.'

'Of course, no problem. And I'm so glad she likes it — truly. I didn't mean to sound so off-hand just now.' He smiled and I forgave him instantly. 'No, leave her to me. And I am grateful, Lindsey. It's very important; else I wouldn't have bothered you. But the editor of an archaeological journal has given me a deadline to meet. When can you start?'

'When? Oh, er, right away of you like. If it's that urgent.'

I spent the next half-an-hour

immersed in pre-history, and contrary to my expectations found the report very interesting and readable. Consequently the sudden strident voice took me completely off-guard and I jumped in surprise. As I turned I discovered Amy standing in the doorway, glowering at me.

'What on earth are you doing in here?'

'I'm typing a report for Nick,' I said in a level voice. 'He told me you had to go and nurse your mother and he wanted it urgently.'

I typed up the remaining few lines that finished the page and pulled it from the machine scanning it for accuracy.

'He'd no business to,' Amy snapped. I looked up in mild surprise. 'I told him I'd be back as soon as I could.' Nastily she added, 'Making yourself indispensable, are you? First you take on his child, now you're worming your way in as his secretary as well.'

I could only goggle at the woman.

Words failed me. Was this was the same person who had been so friendly at first? If I hadn't already discovered about Amy's obsession with Nick, I'd have said what I thought of her. But as things stood, I nearly laughed out loud when I realised that she was jealous. Jealous of me! 'If that's what you want to think Amy, I can't stop you, but you only need ask Nick yourself if you want the truth.'

'Ask Nick what?' came a deep voice from outside the door. 'Oh Amy — you're back,' he said as he entered the room. 'I didn't expect you yet. How's your mother now?'

'She's much better. I left a neighbour sitting with her while I came back to type your report,' she bridled, lifting a shoulder. She was wearing skintight leggings today and a wide-necked knitted cotton sweater of navy-blue. I watched her sidle up to Nick and provocatively smooth down her hair. 'And what do I find?' she hissed at him, 'I needn't have bothered.'

'I asked Lindsay to do it as it has to go off today,' was Nick's mild reply. Not a bit put out, he had completely ignored the side-show and was scanning the pages I handed him. 'Thanks for hurrying back Amy, but I didn't expect you, you see?'

'Well, I know when I'm not wanted.' Amy turned on her heel and flounced out of the room.

'Oh dear, I didn't mean to upset her,' I said, not really caring one way or the other.

'You didn't. It was just a misunderstanding, and all my fault. Don't worry,' Nick said cheerfully, 'She'll get over it. Thanks for doing this,' he gathered up the report and reached for an envelope. 'I'll get it in the post right away.'

★ ★ ★

I awoke next morning with a throbbing headache. All through the time I spent with Emma at her lessons I was conscious of it to a greater or lesser degree at the back of my eyes. And the flashing lights and electronic bleeping of the child's computer did nothing to help. Even when I went outside for a breather, the fresh air didn't shift it; neither did the paracetamol I found in the bathroom cupboard.

I met Jessica in the kitchen when I took Emma to find some lunch. 'Mrs Penwarne,' I said to her, 'is there a chemist in the village?'

'Chemist? No, there's only the post office.' She turned from the worktop and looked at me over her shoulder. 'Why, what did you want?'

'Oh, I've got this stupid headache. I just can't get rid of it. I've tried everything I can think of. I need something stronger.'

Jessica paused with her hand on a cupboard door and said, 'I've just had an idea. Why don't you go and see Mina? She lives in the village. She's an expert on herbal remedies and I'm sure she could give you something for your headache. She's very well-known around here, lots of the local people go to her.'

'Really? Well, it would save me a journey,' I replied, inwardly sceptical. I'd spent too much time in professional medical circles to have much faith in holistic cures. 'Where does she live?'

'Four doors up from the post office, on the same side. Tell her I sent you,' she added.

'Thanks, I will. In fact I'll go right after lunch. I shouldn't be very long, but perhaps someone could keep an eye on Emma until I get back.'

'Of course. I'll see to it. Don't feel you need to hurry back.' Jessica withdrew her head and closed the door again.

Well, I thought, that's the most friendly and helpful she's been in all the weeks I've been here. Perhaps she's thawing out at last.

I found the cottage easily enough and the door was opened by a woman wearing a floating sleeveless gown of ethnic pattern in subdued earth colours — sludgy greens, ochre and brown over a yellow shirt.

'Hello, you're Mina, aren't you?' I said with a smile. 'Jessica Penwarne sent me to you. She said you supply herbal medicines.'

'Come inside,' said Mina. Her face was expressionless and her eyes were clear and almost colourless. Like glass, or river water. They swept over me as she waved a hand and directed me down a passage to a room at the back of the cottage.

'I've got this dreadful headache which won't go away. I've had it for a couple of days now. I suppose it must be the stress,' I added to myself without thinking, then wished I hadn't as Mina fastened on to it.

'What kind of stress?' she queried, with a lift of her straight black brows.

How about finding that my employer whom I liked and trusted, and who I thought was as open and honest as the day, is dressing up and 'haunting' the neighbourhood for who knows what reasons of his own?

'Oh,' I improvised, 'it's the worry over Emma — you know, the child I look after. The responsibility. I do so want her to get her voice back.'

'You need to learn how to relax.' With the brief reply, Nina rose to her feet and began systematically grinding some kind of vegetation to death in the pestle. 'I hold classes down at the Whole-Being Centre, in the village hall on Wednesday afternoons. You should come. Three o'clock to four every week.'

'I'll think about it,' I replied cautiously.

'Meanwhile, you could start drinking herbal tea instead of poisoning your system with caffeine.' Nina reached down a box which contained an assortment of packets and pushed it towards me. 'Camomile, rosemary, hyssop, mistletoe and lime blossom.' She intoned the names like a litany. 'These will sooth away your tensions and lead to deep, restful sleep.'

7

I slept fairly well and awoke with a clear head after trying the herbal teas and decided to take another one next morning. I was making up one of the flowery brews when Jessica arrived in the kitchen.

'How are you feeling today?' she enquired. Taller than me by a couple of inches, and rigidly straight-backed, she looked down her long nose as she spoke.

I met the cool grey eyes with a smile. 'Much better, I'm glad to say — touch wood,' I added, tapping the bread bin.

'You're superstitious, are you?'

'Pardon?' I must have gaped at her with sheer incomprehension.

'Touching wood,' Jessica explained. 'It comes from the primitive custom of touching trees for good luck. Ancient people used to believe that good spirits lived in trees, you see.'

'Oh,' I said blankly, 'I didn't know that. It's something everyone says without thinking.'

'Quite. So did Mina give you something to take?' Jessica seemed in no hurry. She folded her arms and leaned against the work-top. I could hardly push past her and leave the room without seeming ill-mannered. Especially as she seemed to be making an effort to be more friendly these days.

'She recommended drinking herbal teas.' I held out the mug for her to see. 'This is one of them. Of course, it could be pure coincidence that my head is so much better.' I shrugged.

Jessica nodded. 'I see.'

'Mina also said I should go to her relaxation classes,' I said.

'Oh yes. On Wednesdays. That's right, isn't it? And it's Wednesday today. Have you decided to go?'

'I think I probably shall,' I replied. 'Well, I must get back to Emma,' I said, drawing away.

Curiosity drove me to the Whole-Being Centre that afternoon and I was surprised to find so many people there. Inside the hall the seats were arranged in a semi-circle and as there were only single spaces left I inserted myself into one of these between a couple of strangers.

Mina appeared almost at once. Today she was wearing a baggy shirt and a plum-coloured waistcoat with fringes, over black trousers.

'Welcome, everyone,' she lowered the hands and clasped them in front of her. 'We'll begin right away as there is rather a lot to get through today. First the usual exercises, designed to clear the mind, relax the body and induce a general feeling of peace and well-being to both the body and the soul. Please close your eyes, empty your mind of all external matters and concentrate on breathing slowly and deeply as I shall tell you.'

I had a quick look around the room and noted that the gathering was made up entirely of women, about twenty or so, mostly 'thirty-somethings', with a few older ones.

'In slowly — hold — and slowly out. In. Out. Again. Good.' The woman's voice was hypnotic. 'Feel the tensions leaving you. Your body is being drained of all the worries, all the stress, all the demands of daily living. You are free. Free to open your spirits to higher things and let peace and the awareness of peace into your minds.'

Silence had fallen. I opened half an eye and peeked at all the rapt faces. The young woman sitting next to me was breathing deeply, a private smile on her lips, her eyes tightly shut. Then I jumped as Mina clapped her hands.

'Right,' she said and a general shuffling and murmuring rippled round the room. 'Remember to make relaxation a part of your daily life and try to find a few minutes each day to give to your inner self.'

Mina gave a brisk nod over her clasped hands and pulled up a chair for herself. Seated, she picked up a sheaf of papers from a nearby table and scanned them, 'Now, notices. Next month there will be courses in aromatherapy and yoga, the dates will be on the board. I'm also hoping to get a speaker soon on the nature and properties of crystals, and if anyone has any ideas or suggestions for other topics I shall be pleased to have them. We'll take a break now and afterwards I have another matter to discuss with you all.'

She stood up and a general burst of chatter broke out. Several women headed towards the kitchen and began clattering cups and saucers. Obviously tea was on the way. I turned towards the person sitting next to me on the right. The woman on my other side had disappeared kitchenwards with the rest.

'Hello,' said my neighbour, 'I haven't seen you here before.' One of the 'thirty-somethings'.

'No, this is the first I've been.'

'I come as often as I can. When the children are at school and I can get away. I really enjoy it, the break and the company. I'm Teresa, by the way.'

'Lindsey,' I said.

'You aren't from round here, are you?' Teresa said, straightening her colourful flowing skirt.

Judging by her local accent, Teresa most certainly was from 'round here' herself. 'No, I came down from London a few months ago to a live-in job. With the Penwarnes — I expect you know them — up at Carn Wartha.'

Teresa hooked a lock of hair behind one ear. 'Oh yes, yes I do. You must be looking after the little girl, are you? I heard they'd got somebody.'

'That's right — '

'Oh, here's the tea,' broke in the garrulous Teresa, 'come on, we fetch our own from the counter. The money goes in that box there.'

I took a cup and hoped Mina wasn't watching. I felt guilty drinking the 'poisonous' caffeine, then annoyed with myself for caring. For goodness sake, I'm a free agent, I told myself crossly. I followed Teresa back to our places and sat down just as Mina reappeared. When everyone had settled down she began without preamble.

'Something rather special has come up,' she announced, 'which I need to discuss with you all. Most of you will have some knowledge of the society called the Board of Cornish Historians. Their aim is to keep alive the spirit of Cornwall by conferring membership of their group on those people they consider have contributed something worthwhile to Cornish culture.'

Several heads around me were nodding and murmuring as she went on, 'Each year they hold their annual rally and ceremonials at a different ancient site in the county. And this year they have chosen Carn Wartha and the Dancing Maidens.'

She paused and looked at us all. 'I can now tell you that we have been asked if we can put on a pageant, something symbolic of the rituals which at one time took place at the stones.

'I consider this to be quite an honour, and I'm relying on you all to help me out by taking part in this project, which we shall be discussing over the next few weeks. It's to be held on Midsummer Eve, which means we haven't a great deal of time, so I've already given it some thought and have come up with a few ideas.'

She paused again and another rustle went round the room, along with a low babble of conversation. 'It sounds quite fun,' Teresa whispered in my ear. 'I'm willing to join in if you are. How about it?'

Why not, I thought. It would be a bit of harmless fun, and fun had been sadly lacking in my life lately. Before I changed my mind, I gave a nod and grinned at Teresa's eager face. 'OK, you're on,' I replied.

'What I thought we might do,' Mina explained, 'is this. The primitive people were sun and moon worshippers. As this ceremony will take place in the evening, I would like to present a scene about the ancient moon culture. This was very involved and would take too long to go into now — we'll leave it until later. But I shall need nine of you as dancers, another three to represent the three ages of womanhood — that is, maiden, mother and crone — and various other helpers on the sidelines. Can you please give me some idea of how many of you are interested by raising your hands?'

About two-thirds of the company did so.

'That's wonderful. Now, rehearsals. As most of you have families to consider, I suggest we meet in the evenings — about 7.30? On Friday of this week and each Friday following, if you agree. Here first of all, and later on at the Stones. Does that suit everybody?'

There was no dissent, so Mina clapped her notebook shut and finished by declaring, 'Right, Friday it is then. Thank you all for your support. I look forward to seeing you at 7.30.' She rose from her seat and began to gather up books and papers as chairs scraped in the body of the hall and a burst of chatter broke out as the meeting dispersed.

8

A spell of perfect weather had set in, and the ribbon of sea visible from my window next morning was a pure forget-me-not blue. The sun cast a golden glow over the bare rocky bones of the land which was clothed now in a robe of grasses and wildflowers swaying in the gentle breeze. With my elbows on the window-sill, I breathed in the scents of summer and vowed to make the most of it.

Amy was below me in the yard hanging out washing and Nick had taken off somewhere for a walk.

'Nick adores Emma, doesn't he?' I remarked to Amy, who was shaking out a bath-towel ready to hang it on the line. 'It's appalling to think that she's all he has left.' I watched him go out of sight and sighed, 'But I do believe she's improving, Amy,' I said, my eyes still on the running child as she followed her father. 'What do you think?'

Amy's mouth was set and her eyes cold as I turned to look at her. 'Mm, perhaps,' came the guarded reply as she swept a shirt from the basket and jabbed it with a couple of pegs.

Of course. I'd forgotten how jealous of me she was, but surely there must be some way of convincing her there was nothing to be jealous about?

'Amy,' I said, 'you seem to think there's something going on between Nick and me. But you're completely wrong, you know.'

I wasn't prepared even then for the virulence in her expression as she glared at me over the rotary line. Two bright flags of colour stained her cheeks and her nostrils flared as she spat, 'I suppose then, that's why you were both sitting in the kitchen the other night — well, one o'clock in the morning's more like it — holding hands!'

She flung a pillow-case back into the

basket at her feet and came round to my side of the line where she stood with her hands on her hips. 'And don't even try to deny it. I saw you. I noticed the light when I was going to bed. I'd stayed up to watch a late film, and came across in case anyone was sick, to see if I could help.'

In case you missed something, more like, I thought. Aloud I said bitterly, 'You've got it entirely wrong, Amy. But you wouldn't believe there was an innocent reason for it, would you?'

'Hah! Too right I wouldn't,' came the retort.

'In that case I won't even try to explain,' I said.

* * *

'You haven't forgotten you've got a rehearsal tonight, have you?' Jessica asked me over the dinner table. 'You told me Friday, didn't you?'

I swallowed and replied, 'Oh no, I'm looking forward to it.'

'This is the entertainment for Midsummer Eve, is it?' Nick enquired and his mother nodded. 'Well,' he went on, pushing aside his plate, 'I've got a bit of news actually.' He fished in a pocket and pulled out an envelope. 'I had this letter today from the Board of Cornish Historians inviting me to attend the ceremony.'

He smoothed out the letter and placed it on the corner of the table. As he glanced down at it, he said with a note of quiet pride in his voice, 'They're offering me membership of their group because of the work I've done at the site. Apparently they think the excavation of the settlement is a major addition to local knowledge of this area and is 'worthy of recognition'.'

'Oh, Nick, that's wonderful!' I exclaimed.

I could tell from his face he was really pleased, and I was genuinely glad for him. He'd spent far more hours on the job than he'd been paid for, to my knowledge, because it was partly a labour of love and the fulfilment of a dream to him, and partly I suspected, because work filled in all the lonely hours that would have been family time in normal circumstances.

'Thank you, Lindsey,' he said with a smile as a slight flush reddened his sun-tanned face.

'And so you should,' said Jessica, bridling, 'it's about time you received some acknowledgement. It's only what you deserve.'

'Well, fancy. All that poking about in the dirt was worth something after all,' drawled Tim. 'What do you get, a medal?'

'A certificate, actually,' replied Nick, 'and I have to take part in the initiation ceremony, unfortunately.'

'Why 'unfortunately'?' I asked.

'Because they all dress up in long robes and head-dresses, a bit like the ancient Druids, you know?'

'You're joking!' I just didn't believe it and I laughed out loud at the very thought.

'I wish I was. There's a lot of symbolism attached to the whole thing. They take it very seriously, and if you accept the honour you have to go through with it.'

'It's all conducted in the Cornish language as well,' Jessica put in importantly.

'The Cornish language?' I said in astonishment.

'Oh, it died out about three hundred years ago,' Nick began to explain, 'but it was revived by some specialist groups.'

'Oh, right. Do you speak it yourself, Nick?'

'Not me. I don't know the first thing about it. I suppose I'll muddle through somehow,' he replied cheerfully, and rose to leave.

★ ★ ★

I pulled up at the centre in good time for the rehearsal and joined the rest of the group already assembled.

Mina lost no time in getting down to

business. 'I shall need nine volunteers for the dancers first. Preferably anyone who has had previous experience of music and movement of any sort, although the steps are very simple.'

'I did some ballet as a kid,' Teresa remarked to me behind her hand.

'So did I actually,' I whispered, but not quietly enough, for Mina overheard us. 'Right, please step to this side,' she said, waving an imperious hand and setting her Indian bracelets jangling.

'I used to do gymnastics,' came another voice.

'So did I . . . ' and very soon Mina had her nine moon maidens.

The plaintive wail of pipe music filled the room, haunting and evocative. Mina in a flowing skirt of jade and turquoise, dipped and twirled gracefully as we carefully watched what she was doing with her feet.

'It doesn't look too complicated, does it? What do you think?' I asked Teresa who was looking over my shoulder.

'No, I reckon I could manage that

with a bit of practice.'

We were soon getting the hang of it and moving well enough together to be left on our own. After a bit we were allowed a rest-break while Mina filled us in with a few more details. We sat about in various positions on the floor.

Mina was still pacing back and forth, holding a notebook in her hand which she frequently consulted.

'The costumes you will be wearing,' she announced, 'are being borrowed from the amateur dramatic society in Penzance. I should be getting them shortly, then you can try them on for size. I don't anticipate any problems as they're only flowing, Grecian-style gowns, but the sooner we get them sorted out the better.'

'And does all this take place inside the stones?' enquired a voice from the far side of the room.

'That's right. The only people allowed inside at all will be the participants. The public are restricted to one side only from which to watch.'

'And where will we be while the first part of the ceremony is going on?' I asked.

'Oh, I forgot to mention that there'll be a marquee on the site for us to change in, and another one where refreshments will be served afterwards.' Mina swung herself to her feet and came to join us. 'Now if there are no other questions, we'll go through the dance steps again and call it a day.'

We eventually dispersed with a babble of chatter and laughter, and I found I was enjoying this unexpected socialising and was really looking forward to the next meeting.

The week passed fairly quickly, and soon we were gathering on the carn for a full-scale rehearsal.

It was a gorgeous evening, mild and still with a sky full of stars and the rehearsal went smoothly and passed without incident. 'Do you want a lift back, Lindsey?' Teresa asked as we finished changing. 'Malcolm's coming for me.'

'Thanks, but no thanks,' I replied. 'I'll enjoy the walk, and it'll do me good.' I felt like a bit of peace and serenity before I went back to Hawk Farm.

★   ★   ★

'Oh, Lindsey, there you are.' Nick looked up from the breakfast table the next morning as Emma and I came in.

Jessica nodded and said, 'Good morning,' a cup of tea poised in her hand.

'I've something to ask you.' He'd obviously been opening his mail, as ripped envelopes and a pile of letters lay beside his plate. He waved one of them at me. 'Sit down and listen to this.'

He indicated the chair next to him, so I slid into it, opposite Emma who immediately helped herself to cereal and began on her breakfast. 'My word,' said her father with a grin, 'you're the hungry one this morning. You can hear this too, Emma. It concerns all of us.

You and Grandma, too.'

The child's big dark eyes fastened on Nick's face. There was interest there and the hint of a smile. I wondered what was coming, too, as I helped myself to coffee. I'd had enough of herbal flavours by now and had regressed to the demon caffeine, so far without ill-effect.

Nick regarded Emma fondly as he went on, 'This letter is from the Cornish Historians — you know, the people who are giving me the presentation on the evening of the pageant?' Emma took another spoonful of cornflakes. 'Well, it seems that they would like my family to play a more leading part in it, in my honour. And that includes you.' He beamed at the little girl. 'You'll do that for me, won't you, sweetheart?'

Emma's brows had drawn together in a frown. She looked down at her plate and stirred its contents round and round, then glanced dubiously at her father. 'Especially,' Nick added, 'if I tell you that both Grandma and Lindsey have been asked to take a special part as well.'

'What?' I exclaimed, 'Mina never mentioned it to me!'

'Mina doesn't know yet. The organisers thought it would be nice to have the three generations of the family involved. My mother, my . . . wife . . . ' his voice dropped to an aside, 'and my daughter. They didn't know, you see, that I'm a — er — widower.' He cleared his throat and turned to me. 'So I wondered, Lindsey, if you would mind stepping in and supporting Emma.'

The little girl turned her head and fastened her eyes on me. 'Nick, this sounds awfully like blackmail to me.' I turned to him with a smile and intercepted an icy glare from Jessica. She'd been about to say something but I'd got in first. 'I'd like to know what I'm letting myself in for before I agree. What do we have to do?'

'Well, I'm not too sure myself,' he replied, reaching for the cornflakes, 'but it's something to do with you three acting out the three phases of the moon — waxing, full and waning.'

'Well, I think it's the height of folly,' cut in Jessica crisply. 'Quite unnecessary, and putting far too much strain on the child, considering her condition.' She placed her cup back on to its saucer with an expressive clink.

I countered, looking her straight in the eye and said, 'As far as Emma is concerned, I think it will do her far more good than harm to have a bit of excitement in her life.'

Jessica gave a sniff and glared at me as Nick cut in. 'The letter goes on to say that they've written to Mina as well, explaining the situation, and she is very happy about it. Besides which,' he turned and held my eyes with his, 'I should very much like you to agree. Please say you will.'

There was such a note of pleading in his voice and his eyes were so heart-stoppingly dark, that all my stiff-necked pride dissolved quite away and I heard myself saying obediently, 'In that case, Nick, of course I will.'

Jessica gave a snort of disgust, rose to her feet and left the room.

★ ★ ★

What had been a wet, blustery and thoroughly unpleasant morning gave way to more settled weather in the afternoon, so Emma and I put on boots and anoraks and set off for a walk along the cliffs. Ben went bounding on ahead, barking with delight at being let off his lead, and Emma scampered after him, throwing sticks which excited him even more.

There was no way I could keep up with that pace, so I ambled along in the rear and left them to tire each other out. Soon both dog and child had rounded the bluff of a hill-slope out of my sight, and I expected them to be waiting for me, sprawled out and exhausted, by the time I caught them up.

Surprisingly, there was no sign of either of them when I did eventually round the bend. The winding track was deserted and there was not the slightest hint of movement anywhere on the vast expanse of open moorland which swept majestically to the sea.

Anxiety began to fan the tiny flicker of doubt which was hovering deep inside me. Something was wrong.

9

There was just no way that a large, boisterous dog and a six-year-old child could disappear from the face of the earth in the five minutes that they had been out of my sight.

Could they have been abducted? But how? No vehicle could have come anywhere near us over this rough terrain even if there had been time to do so.

Don't be a fool, I told myself. They're hiding somewhere, and Emma's making Ben keep quiet until they're found. You should be glad she's improved to the extent of playing hide and seek. Think of the withdrawn little figure she used to be, and how different she is now.

I tried to convince myself, but churning away in the pit of my stomach was a growing knot of fear. How could I possibly face the family — Nick, Jessica, any of them, but especially Nick — if I had to confess I'd failed to keep an eye on Emma because I was simply too lazy to keep up with her? How feeble it would sound. And how could I live with myself if something dreadful had happened to her?

I then took a deep breath and forced myself to swallow down my rising panic. What should I do? Run back to Hawk Farm and raise the alarm? But if Emma was in danger I might be wasting valuable time.

I began to shout then. Calling first her name, then whistling up the dog. I lurched off the path and plunged into the knee-high heather and bracken. Thorns tore at my legs from the scrubby gorse and brambles in the undergrowth, but I didn't even feel them.

My voice was growing hoarse as I yelled and shouted even louder, screaming Emma's name into the wind, even though I knew all the time that she couldn't call back, but the wind just blew it mockingly back in my face.

What about the dog? Surely if Emma was hurt in some way, Ben would come back to fetch me? He was so devoted to her and was such an intelligent animal.

All I could see in my mind's eye was both child and dog lying at the bottom of the cliff.

I would have to go and look over, and steel myself for what I might see below. My breath was coming in great ragged sobs now as I forced my weary legs through the myriad clinging stems of lush summer undergrowth. Several times I tripped and fell, lacerating my hands on the thorns of the low-growing burnet roses which covered the heath.

Then distantly, indistinctly, I heard the bark of a dog. Never had anything sounded so welcome. Two short, sharp barks. Ben! I summoned up my last bit of strength and scrambled to my feet.

'Ben,' I cried, 'Ben, where are you? Come here, here boy, come.' It came out as a croak, but I could hear an answering bark and my spirits lifted another notch.

The dog's bark sounded closer, but strangely muffled. I stopped and listened. A burst of continuous and excited barking was coming now, somewhere to my right, I was sure. And coming from underneath the ground!

My heart began thumping wildly as I scanned the nearby undergrowth. There was a stand of scrubby bushes not far off and I gingerly pushed my way through them, hanging on to their tough and sinewy branches in case I fell into whatever hole Ben seemed to be in.

Once through this curtain of growth, I found myself in a shallow, grass-covered depression in the ground. Roughly circular in shape, it was slick with damp and extremely slippery. I kept my grip on the bushes and called the dog again.

A frantic barking came from the centre of the pit, where another stand of bushes grew, smaller ones which apparently covered the hole down which the dog had fallen — and Emma? Oh, please yes, I silently prayed, as I pondered what to do next.

And then I saw it, like a miracle. Like an answer to a prayer. There was a rope there — a real, strong, honest-to-goodness rope, firmly knotted to the strongest of bushes and reaching down to the centre of the pit, where it disappeared in the undergrowth.

I didn't stop to wonder about the hows and whys of it being there. I seized it and cautiously launched myself downward, digging in my heels to steady myself as I went. I could stand upright again when I reached the middle, so still keeping hold of the rope with one hand, I bent down and peered through the leaves.

'Ben!' I called once more and was nearly deafened by a crescendo of barking just below me, but that was not all. As the dog stopped to draw breath, I heard another voice. Someone was calling my name. Dizzily I stared into the blackness. 'Lindsey, Lindsey, please come and get me, quickly,' came a plaintive cry.

'Emma?' I called incredulously, as my heart beat a wild tattoo against my ribs, almost drowning out the sound. 'Emma, is that really you?'

'Get me out of here,' came the reply and a torrent of sobs came echoing upward.

'Sweetheart, don't worry, I'm on my way. Here I come, don't cry. You'll soon be safe.'

My hands were shaking so much I could hardly grasp the rope, but I gritted my teeth and launched myself forward and down, to land in a heap on the dry shale floor of a large cave.

'Emma, darling!' She flung herself into my outstretched arms and we both burst into tears. We clung together for several minutes before I fished a wad of tissues from a pocket and mopped us both up. At last I had recovered enough to say, 'Your voice! You're speaking again! At last!'

Emma sniffed and scrubbed at her

eyes. 'It came back,' she said simply. 'When I heard you calling, I wanted to call, too. So I tried and tried, and after a bit, I just did.' She thrust the crumpled tissue at me and drew away. 'Can we go home now? I'm hungry.'

I couldn't move for a moment. I just sat there on the floor while waves of dizziness and nausea threatened to overwhelm me. my entire body ached, I was scratched and bruised all over and so dead-weary I wondered how I was ever going to find the strength to get us all out of this place, but inside, my heart was singing like a bird. Emma was all right. And more than all right. She was actually speaking.

'We will in just a minute after I've had a tiny rest. Come and sit beside me and tell me what happened.'

Emma curled up on my lap and Ben sat on his haunches and regarded us solemnly, as she began, 'I put Ben on his lead to come back to you, because I was tired but he didn't want to come. Then a rabbit jumped out from under a bush and he ran after it and dragged me with him. We tumbled down a slope and landed in this cave. I hurt my knees, look.' Emma's bottom lip began to tremble and tears were in her eyes again as I hugged her tightly and dabbed at the scraped knees with a tissue.

'They'll soon be better,' I assured her, shuddering to think of how easily she could have broken a limb. 'You've had an adventure, like Alice in Wonderland falling down the rabbit hole!' and she gave a watery smile. 'Now we've got to find a way of getting out of here.'

'There's the rope,' she said, 'I can climb out with the rope, Lindsey.'

'So can I,' I added, 'but Ben can't.'

I'd been having a good look around the cave as we'd been talking, and now realised the sooner we got out of it the better. There were two cigarettes ends on the floor, which along with the rope, indicated that someone made a habit of coming here and I didn't want to be around the next time he did so.

'Now, what I think we'll do,' I said aloud, 'is to make a pile of these big flat stones for Ben to climb on, so he can reach the opening. Then if I stand on top of them as well, I can give him a push and I'm pretty sure he'll be able to scramble out.' Once he was that far, I was hoping the dog could claw his way up the grassy slope by himself.

'Oh, yes. Come on, let's start.' Emma jumped to her feet and together we shifted several large stones and piled them up beneath the opening above. It wasn't a big drop, just too far for the dog to leap on his own.

'Now, Emma, I'll climb up first and call to him, then I'll be there ready to give him a push if he needs it. You stand by then, for your turn.'

The great dog seemed to know exactly what was expected of him and managed his escape far more easily than I'd anticipated.

'You next, Emma,' I called. 'Grab the other end of the dog lead, here you are,' as I handed it to her. 'Now climb on to the stones and I'll give you a pull to help you up.' I steadied myself against the cave wall and guided her to my side.

'Good girl. That's the first part. Now I want you to take hold of the rope and pull yourself right up to the top of the slope. Dig your heels into the grass as you go. I'll hold this end and keep it steady for you. OK? Off you go.'

I made it sound as simple as I could, but my heart was in my mouth as she began to swing about in mid-air before getting her feet planted on the edge of the opening. I was also taking the strain of her weight as I hung grimly on to the end of the rope. But she was an agile little girl and was soon shouting gleefully down to me. 'I'm up, Lindsey, I'm up! Come on!'

I made a wry face and looked urgently around for somewhere to anchor the rope. If I could fasten the end of it securely it would make my ascent so much easier. I looped it round a projecting rock and tried to remember all I'd ever learned in the Girl Guides about tying knots.

It must have been enough, or else good luck was on my side, for in a few moments I joined the others on the cliff top, where I lay gasping like a stranded fish, my breath coming in great tearing gasps.

And now we must head for home and spread the good news to the rest of the family.

As we went, I let myself think properly about the miraculous return of Emma's speech. It must have been shock treatment — the shock of the sudden fall had brought it back as surely as shock had caused her to lose it in the first place.

It also occurred to me somewhat later, after the excitement was over, that in the light of Emma's recovery I would soon presumably, be out of a job. This realisation prompted mixed feelings within me. Regret that — yes, admit it — I should never see Nick Penwarne again. Or indeed, Emma. I'd become very fond of the little girl while she had been in my care.

There were two things I was determined to do however, and soon. One was to return to the cave that Emma had fallen into and discover who had provided the rope we had used to get us out. The other was to find out what Nick, the ghostly joker on the hill, was playing at.

The perfect opportunity presented itself a few days later. Emma had gone up to Truro for a check-up with the specialist who had originally been in charge of her case and was being kept in overnight for observation. She would now, we hoped and expected, be discharged from medical care.

So as I had a free morning, I whistled up the dog and set off across the open moor. It was a lazy summer day, just made for basking in the sun and doing nothing.

I made straight for the stand of bushes which I knew concealed the grassy dip where the cave entrance was, and pushed through them. There was no convenient rope hanging there today and I had to slither and slip down to the heather-covered hole, clutching at roots and tufts of grass to stop myself falling in as Emma had done.

I steadied myself on the edge and peered inside. It was deserted, so I jumped down with Ben following at my heels and took a good look around. The cave was the size of a smallish room, funnelling at the back to a passage which sloped downwards and out of sight. A surprising amount of light filtered in slantwise through the entrance, particularly on this sunny morning.

On the floor were several discarded cigarette stubs, which I had noticed before, and there were footprints in the dust, trodden over and into each other as if this hideaway was frequently used.

Ben had gone snuffling towards the back of the cave and was part-way down the passage, wagging his tail at some interesting scent he had picked up. I followed him and the first thing that caught my eye was a natural shelf in the rocky wall where a variety of things had been stowed neatly away, providing even more proof that this place was frequently used by somebody. There were candles there and matches, a vacuum flask and a powerful torch. Also a bundle of dark material had been rolled up and stuffed into a corner.

I wonder . . . I took it down and shook out the folds. As I thought — a man's black dressing-gown with a hood, exactly like a monk's habit, even to the cord tie around the waist. Here in my hand was all the proof I needed of my cigarette-smoking ghost.

I might as well explore the rest of the passage having come this far, and see where it led. I put Ben on the lead and let him guide me, as the light was growing very faint as we went further away from the entrance. The path sloped downwards, with gritty shale underfoot.

However, we hadn't gone more than a few yards when I was surprised to find it getting lighter again. I could also hear the sea. So, it must lead right down to the beach. Interesting — a smugglers' cave, perhaps? There were supposed to be plenty of those in Cornwall by all accounts.

Deep in thought, I was suddenly brought up sharp against a solid wall of rock as we reached the opening and I could see the sky above my head. Ben was barking with excitement as he caught the smells of the seashore, and I let him loose as I searched for a way out. The dog found it before I did, a narrow slit just big enough to squeeze through, and we emerged on to a high, rocky plateau a few feet above the cove.

The sun was directly in my eyes but in spite of this, I could see a flight of natural steps leading down to the beach. And up these steps was climbing a familiar figure, straight towards me and the cave mouth and there was no way I was going to avoid a face-to-face confrontation with him.

It's surprising how much can go

through your mind in a second or two when the adrenaline soars. What should I do? To go back through the cave would make me feel foolish when he caught me up, especially so if he — I had to face it — decided to turn nasty.

Nick? Oh, Nick — I couldn't believe it of him. But if I had found out his secret? Face to face with him here I would have to squeeze past him before I could run, and Ben, great shambling, amiable animal, was useless, being at the other end of the beach by now and totally unaware of anything except the enticing smells along the tideline.

I stood there feeling very vulnerable. Nick had seen me emerging from the hidden entrance, therefore I must have been through the cave and found the secret hiding-place containing his disguise. I'd blown his cover.

He came to a halt and was standing a few yards from me looking — how? Apprehensive? Guilty? Embarrassed? But certainly not violent. I realised I'd been holding my breath all the time

I'd been watching him get nearer and nearer. Now I let it out in a long sigh of relief and looked him squarely in the face.

As he came closer my stomach did a flip and a whole lot of answers clicked into place inside my head. The resemblance was unmistakable.

Here was an older Nick, in features, in build, in the way he moved and as he ran his fingers through his hair in the gesture I knew so well, in mannerisms, too.

'You're Marcus!' I exclaimed.

'How do you know? Who are you? What are you doing here?' he blustered, but made no attempt to deny it.

'I think we need to talk,' I replied. I felt completely in control now and all my former nervousness had flown. But I didn't fancy being alone with him in an underground tunnel, miles from anywhere, so I sat down on a flat slab where I was and he went to do the same.

'How did you discover the cave?' he

asked, sinking down heavily on to a low rock just opposite, and looking warily at me.

'It's a long story,' I replied. I told him who I was and then launched into the tale of Emma's accident.

'It's actually an old mine adit,' Marcus said as I finished.

'A what?'

'An adit is a drainage shaft — in a mine. Or an air passage. There were exploratory diggings for tin around here years ago, when I was a boy, but they didn't come to much. That's when I found the cave myself.'

'So why are you playing at ghosts on Carn Wartha and scaring off the local people.' Not Nick! Not Nick, my heart was singing.

Marcus looked down at his feet and scuffed a toe in some blown sand. 'That's an even longer one.' He paused and heaved a sigh. 'It began twenty years ago. But I'll give you the gist of it.'

Marcus fumbled in a pocket and drew out a packet of cigarettes. 'Do you . . . ?' I shook my head. He lit his own and blew a spiral of blue smoke. He watched it rise, then keeping his eyes on the sky where woolly clouds of fantastic shapes marched in stately procession across the upper air, said, 'It's rather ironic really, that I should have been discovered now, after all this time, because I've finished what I came to do, you see. The night you saw me was probably the last.'

'But what were you doing?' I snapped.

He leaned forward, elbows on knees and flicked some ash on to the rocks. Then, keeping his eyes down, he went on, 'When I left Jessica and the children, Lindsey, I was so uptight I didn't know what to do or where to go. Over a long period she had immersed herself in the demands of the other children, and the house and farm. To the extent that she had no time for me and no understanding of my feelings in those days.

'I tried — heaven knows I tried

— but I just was not cut out to be a farmer, and she adamantly refused to do anything else — like moving away from here and making a fresh start.' Marcus hunched his shoulders and his expression was so defeated that I found myself feeling sorry for him.

'Well, a man can only take so much.' He straightened up and leaned his back against a comfortable boulder. 'I walked out, as you know, and the longer I stayed away the harder it was to come back or even to make contact at all. I deserted them, Lindsey, my wife and three little sons and left them to fend for themselves. And the longer I stayed away, the shame of doing so added to the guilt I felt already, and formed a barrier which I couldn't break through.' He lowered his eyes and stubbed out the cigarette.

He gave me a rueful smile. 'I suppose in these enlightened days we would both have had 'counselling' and all that stuff. But at that time people were left to sort out their own problems in their own way. As it was, the years went on . . . and well, there we are.'

'I'm trying to understand how you must have felt,' I said at last, 'and yes, I agree that Jessica should have come halfway to meet you and patch up your differences. But, Marcus,' I spread both palms in a gesture of bewilderment, 'I can't imagine how you could have stayed away so long, with no news of them, nor they of you. They didn't even know if you were dead or alive.'

Marcus hung his head and looked at his feet as he seemed lost in his memories. Eventually his head snapped up and he glared at me from under furrowed brows. 'No-one who hasn't been through it should presume to judge,' he growled, then added in his own defence, 'I did have a source of news, as much news as I wanted, and I sent Jessica money when I could spare it. Anonymously, of course, but she must have known who it came from.'

'Anyway, what did you do when you left here? Where did you go?' I asked.

'Initially I went to Plymouth, caught the ferry to Roscoff and tramped about France wondering whether to commit suicide and end it all, but I was too much of a coward for that as well,' he said bitterly.

Marcus took a deep breath and opened his palms as he prepared to speak. 'To begin with I made a living out of teaching English,' he went on, 'and then I began studying on my own account — something I'd always wanted to do. I became fluent in French and read physics and astronomy to university level. I'd always been interested in standing stones and Brittany is full of them. Over the years, I travelled all over Europe and eventually I became quite an authority on Celtic lore and wrote several books on the subject, which were very well received.'

He had become more animated now and his face brightened as he began to enlarge on his favourite topic. 'More recently I've started studying the cult of moon worship which involved the stone circles, and I had to come back here because the Dancing Maidens are such an important part of that culture.'

Now I began to see where all this might be leading, but I didn't want to interrupt the flow.

Marcus stood up and stretched, then leaned a foot on a smooth step of rock worn out of the cliff by the constant erosion of salt and weather, and looked out to sea.

'You can probably work out the rest of it for yourself,' he went on. 'I had to use a disguise for several reasons. One being that I naturally couldn't risk anyone recognising me and telling my family. I didn't want passing walkers asking stupid questions either, when I was trying to work.' He turned back to me and added over his shoulder, 'So I took advantage of an old legend and became a ghost.'

'But — where do you live?' I asked him, 'not down here, surely?' I gestured towards the cave and his belongings.

'Good Lord, no, I've got a flat in Truro. I leave the car on the other side of the village and cut across the beach. Hardly ever meet a soul.' He smiled and thrust both hands in his pockets as he turned to face me. 'I only came back now to get some sketches I left behind. I must go in and get them.'

I followed him up through the tunnel, more at ease now that I could see he posed me no threat.

When we had returned to the cave, Marcus reached into a crevice and drew out a roll of cartridge paper. 'There, you see?' He unrolled one sheet and showed me. It was covered with intricate pen and ink diagrams of the sky at night, with the alignments of the stones meticulously drawn in careful detail with a neatness which left me marvelling.

'They're lovely,' I said with sincerity.

Marcus rolled the papers up and slumped down on to a slab of rock again. He sighed and his eyes were far away. 'And at last the wheel has turned full circle,' he said.

I thought he was talking about the drawings until he added, 'Lindsey, I'm in a quandary.' Our eyes locked as I said, 'Oh?' and waited for him to go on.

'You know that Nick has won this honour and is having a special award?' I must have looked surprised, because he remarked, 'Oh, I've been following his career more closely than he'll ever know. Our interests have taken a similar path. And Lindsey, I'm so proud of him.' His eyes misted. 'The awkward thing is,' Marcus paused and took a deep breath, 'that I've been asked to present it to him.'

'What? You?' My jaw dropped.

'Yes. No-one knows we're related, you see. I've been calling myself Mark Warner since I left here.'

'Are you going to do it?' My mind boggled at the implications.

'I'm scared stiff,' admitted Marcus, 'but my mind is made up. I have to do it.' His chin came up. 'I've skulked in the shadows too long. It's time I faced the music, Lindsey. Faced Jessica, faced the children who are now strangers to me, and plead for their forgiveness. In public if need be.'

I had to admire his courage. 'Marcus,' I said into the silence that had fallen, 'what did you mean just now when you said you had a 'source' of news about your family while you were away?'

He looked startled. 'Did I say that?' Oh. Through Mina Rowe. I suppose you've come across her?'

'Mina?' I felt my eyebrows rise to my hairline.

'Yes. I know her parents well. They and I were children together. I came across her in Paris soon after I left here. She was about twenty then and a student at the Sorbonne. We were both visiting an exhibition about Celtic culture. At first I thought my cover had been blown, but Mina is an independent spirit and respects that in other people. She promised to keep my secret and send me news of my family.'

10

We had had one last rehearsal for the pageant up on Carn Wartha, and on the day of the performance Emma was as excited as a cat with two tails. I was fervently hoping it wouldn't all be too much for her. The programme had been slightly altered and now the dancing would come before the awards ceremony, so with a bit of luck she could go home to bed after that. But her face fell and her eyes filled with tears at the very suggestion.

'O-oh no, Lindsey, please,' she begged. 'I want to see Daddy get his prize. Please let me stay!'

It would have taken a heart of stone to refuse her, and I suppose it was being a bit unfair, so I neatly passed the buck and said, 'Well, we'll have to ask Daddy and see what he thinks,' knowing full well that Nick would let her.

He was a different man since Emma's recovery. Most of the stress lines had been ironed out of his brow, he laughed more readily and was more relaxed than I'd ever seen him. I'd been attracted before, of course, but now I had a job to tear my eyes away from him. Nick spent all his spare time with Emma, and consequently with me.

I had the burden of Marcus' secret to carry round with me — at least for a few more days. What effect his reappearance was going to have on the family I could only imagine.

I longed to confide in Nick, being with him so much it was increasingly difficult to act normally. I was in an almost permanent black mood and had to restrain myself more than once from snapping at him.

The important day dawned fine and clear and the weather held all day. By evening the air was mellow with retained warmth and a lazy breeze drifted over Carn Wartha, stirring the long blue gowns and head-dresses of the historical society as they waited in their seats around the outside of the stone circle.

I stood in my place at one of the quarter points of the circle — the northern one. I was keeping a watchful eye on Emma in the south, who in spite of her excitement, was composed and as still as a statue, head up, back straight. Her ankle-length white dress was the same design as my red one and Jessica's black.

I was feeling immensely proud of Emma tonight. Some of my depression had lifted and I now gave myself due credit for the part I'd played in her recovery. I had done the job I'd come here to do. I had roused her from the withdrawn state she'd been in — the shock of the fall had just been the climax of it all.

Behind us both, Jessica stood at the western point, holding like Emma and me, a posy of sweet-smelling herbs. Mina in a gown of shining silver, was

174

standing due east facing the rising moon.

Then a trill of recorder music announced that the pageant was beginning. Into the circle came the dancers, gracefully weaving in and out, their white gowns shimmering in the fading light. And like a backcloth to the whole ceremony, dwarfing its participants, reared the Dancing Maidens of stone, frozen in time, performing to their own silent music.

When we met in the middle we raised our posies high, then tossed them into a large copper dish on the ground and stood around it as Mina lit a taper and touched it to them.

Directly on cue, as if she had conjured it up, a full moon of shimmering silver appeared from behind a towering crag and filed the arena with light. It was spectacular, pure magic, and brought a soft chorus of 'oohs' and 'ahs' from the watching crowds in the shadows. For at that moment I could see how it must have been here thousands of years ago, in the dawn of time beneath the shadow of these same great stones. It was an ancient and utterly pagan moment.

The pageant was over, we acknowledged the applause from the audience in the shadows and filtered into the seats reserved for us. As we passed them, the members of the historical society were rising to join their procession into the circle.

'Well done, Emma!' Nick said as he went by, bending to give her a hug. 'You were perfect.' The child, looking like a small pale moth in her glimmering white dress, threw her arms around his neck and kissed him. I thought of the reserved and silent little girl of not so long ago and swallowed the lump in my throat.

'You do look funny in that long dress, Daddy, and a headscarf!' she giggled, tugging at his headdress. Nick looked rueful and his teeth gleamed white in the shadows as he grinned at me. His eyes looked dark and mysterious as they looked deeply into mine and he said 'Well done,' again, to me this time, but whether he meant Emma's recovery or my performance I wasn't sure.

It was a moment of surprising closeness considering the throng of people around us, and my heart turned over with what? Yearning? Longing? Regret that I should soon be gone?

'Good luck with the speech in Cornish,' I whispered after him and he gave a 'thumbs up' as he took his place among the other blue-robed figures.

Torches in tall sconces had been placed around the inside of the circle and now that these were lighted I could see Marcus sitting at a table with some other dignitaries, waiting to present the awards.

I was sitting in the front row so that Emma could have a good view, and as I turned my head to throw a coat over my shoulders, I discovered that John and Amy, as well as Tim with Jessica, were ranged in the row behind me. All the Penwarnes in fact had turned out to watch Nick receive his award.

There had been a fanfare and an introductory speech by the president, then the enrolment of some new members. Now the award ceremony had begun. I saw Marcus getting to his feet and heard the president introducing him to the assembled company — as 'Mark Warner'. I was the only one present who knew his real identity. Then individual names were called to come forward in turn for their presentations.

It was actually getting pretty boring. I didn't know any of the long string of prizewinners and the incomprehensible language made it worse. Beside me Emma had been wriggling and fidgeting in her seat for some time, before at last she opened her mouth in a massive yawn.

When I saw that Nick's turn was coming my stomach did a flip of excitement. 'Look — Daddy's on next.' I pointed.

Nick was approaching the group at

the table, a sheaf of notes clutched in one hand. Marcus was holding a large silver trophy, the biggest of the evening, in both hands.

He had smartened himself up with a haircut and a good suit, but I could hear the note of nervousness in his voice as he began to speak and recalled how he'd said he was dreading this moment.

'Fellow members of the society, ladies and gentlemen,' he said and cleared his throat, 'First of all I would like to thank you for inviting me here today, and also thank the performers of the pageant for their splendid entertainment. It has been a privilege to present so many hard-earned awards this evening, and I congratulate each and every one of you on your individual achievements.

'However, the highest award of all has still to be presented. The Trevanion Cup is given annually to the member of our society who has made the most significant contribution in that year to

Cornish culture in any of its fields.'

He paused and I could see his hands were shaking by the slight movement of the trophy as it winked in the candlelight.

'This is a very special moment for me personally,' Marcus went on, 'and I would ask you to bear with me briefly while I explain why this is so.'

He drew in a breath and his eyes sought out the audience at the perimeter of the circle, coming finally to rest on the Penwarne family seats.

'Many years ago I lived in this district with my wife and children, but circumstances forced me to take a coward's way out, which I have regretted ever since, and so help me God,' he stifled a sob, 'I deserted them.

'When I was asked to come here tonight I almost took the coward's way again and declined, but at last I'm through with running and I vowed to take this opportunity to apologise, in public, for all the hurt I have caused my family, especially my wife, and ask her whether she can find it in her heart to forgive me, in due course, for my treatment of her.

'Meanwhile,' he clasped the trophy to him and freed a hand to wipe away a tear, 'it gives me untold pride and pleasure to present the Trevanion Cup to Nicholas Penwarne — my son.'

Nick's papers fluttered to the ground as the shock hit him and I could see from where I was sitting, the incredulity on his face. He pulled himself together with remarkable aplomb however and received the cup in a hand that scarcely trembled. The other hand gripped his father's outstretched one and then Marcus pulled Nick to him in a bear-hug.

The audience was on its feet, clapping and cheering, and I stole a swift glance at Jessica behind me. She looked frozen to the spot, her face white as a sheet, one hand clapped across her mouth in disbelief.

There was no time for her or any of us to dwell on this remarkable turn of events, however, before the second bombshell of the evening exploded.

Beside Jessica sat Amy and next to her, on the end of the row, John was sitting. As I turned to face the front again, out of the corner of my eye I caught a flicker of movement.

John was on his feet. Suddenly, John went bolting across the grass into the middle of the arena, shouting and swearing as he went, until he pulled up just short of Marcus and Nick.

They both looked so taken aback they froze where they were, Nick clutching his trophy, Marcus standing in front of the table.

All around us, people were craning their necks to see what was happening, and a babble of chattering had broken out.

'Right, Ladies and Gentlemen,' John was bawling at the top of his voice. 'You've listened to my cowardly louse of a father — now you can listen to me. He didn't tell you the other half of it. About who was left to run the farm practically single-handed from the time he was strong enough to carry a bucket. About his youngest son.' He beat his chest. 'That was me. The one who wasn't clever enough to go to college. The one who wasn't arty enough to paint pictures.

'Good old John, who kept the farm going. Who kept the roof over our heads for nearly twenty years. And never a word of praise or appreciation for it.'

He took a step nearer to Marcus and all at once shot out a hand and grabbed him by his collar and tie. Nick suddenly came to life and dropped his trophy on the table. He reached out a hand to the back of John's neck in an attempt to drag him away from Marcus, but it took the combined strength of both his brother and two other members of the committee to bring John under control as he continued to shout and swear at his father.

Eventually however, he went limp in their grasp and dissolved into noisy tears, allowing them to drag him to the sidelines and out of public view.

At last the police arrived, summoned by somebody's mobile phone. John had been whisked off under escort and Marcus was receiving first-aid. The dramatic events of this evening would keep the village in gossip for a long, long time to come.

11

It was inevitable that Marcus should come back to Hawk Farm with us to recover from his injuries. The fact that Marcus was now dependent on Jessica, and the way in which they had been suddenly thrown together, in a way lessened the shock of his reappearance for her. After a couple of nights on the sofa downstairs she installed him temporarily in the annex, with Amy's permission.

Amy had gone down to the village to stay with her mother until John's future was decided. At the moment he was being detained in a psychiatric hospital undergoing assessment.

'So after I've left, Marcus will be able to have my room,' I remarked to Nick one evening as we sat with our after-dinner coffee in the lounge.

Nick shot me a look of — surprise?

Dismay? I couldn't tell. 'Left?' he echoed, 'You — you're leaving?'

It was my turn to look surprised. 'Of course I am. I've finished the job I came to do. Emma's completely recovered.'

'Where will you go, Lindsey? Do you have any plans?' Nick's eyes were on the cup in his hand and he stirred his coffee slowly round and round.

'Er — no. Not exactly.' I didn't tell him I hadn't the faintest idea where I was going, and was actually feeling more rootless at that moment than at any time in my entire life. 'Back to London, I expect,' I said with more confidence than I felt.

'When are you thinking of going?'

'Soon. Within the next day or two.'

Nick was looking closely at me, then all at once he put down his cup and rose to his feet. 'Come for a walk across the moor, Lindsey?' he said abruptly.

The evening was warm and still and the sea as calm as a millpond. The coast road was deserted and lit by a low moon which rose over the horizon as we watched, then hung in the velvety sky like a great copper plate against the backdrop of the Milky Way. It was a night just made for romance, I thought sadly.

We strolled along the quiet clifftop. The scent of grasses warm with remembered sunshine drifted on the air, and high above us the Dancing Maidens peeped coyly down, their heads veiled in a misty violet gauze.

Nick's hands were stuffed into his pockets and his cream shirt glimmered in the half-light. The track was uneven and just too narrow to walk comfortably side by side, so after we had stumbled against each other several times with murmured apologies, Nick took my arm and tucked it companionably into his own.

'What I wanted to say,' Nick began after a minute or two, 'Was, well, I've noticed since you've been with us that sometimes you've seemed . . . upset, unhappy, worried about Emma perhaps? And I've been so busy that I've never got round to asking you if you were all right.'

He turned to meet my eyes and his own were gleaming in the moonlight, and full of concern. 'I wondered whether it was something I said? I've a lot on my mind but that's no excuse for neglecting other people. And I wanted to apologise, before you go, if it did happen to be my fault, and get it cleared up.'

I almost burst into tears, my emotions were in such a jumble, but I managed to restrain myself and exclaimed, 'Oh, Nick, no! It was never your fault, any of it.' I shook my head firmly as I tried to explain to him how I had seized hold of the wrong end of the stick. 'I've only myself to blame — but I thought it was you up there haunting Carn Wartha for your own nefarious reasons!'

Looking into his surprised face as I faltered to the end of the story, I couldn't suppress a giggle at how ridiculous the whole thing sounded now, and soon we were both roaring with laughter.

Nick put a large warm hand over one of mine and squeezed it. The hand was very comforting. I was in no hurry to draw mine away, but after a few minutes when we each drifted off into thoughts of our own, Nick pulled me to my feet and we began to retrace our steps back to the farm.

★   ★   ★

I was passing the study the next morning when Nick put his head round the door and beckoned me in.

'Come on in, Lindsey. Sit down.' Nick indicated the typing chair. He smiled and perched himself on the corner of the table beside me. He was looking happier than I ever remembered.

'You're looking very pleased with yourself,' I remarked, returning his

189

smile. 'How's Marcus today?'

'Very much better. A bit stiff and bruised, but OK, really.'

'Oh, good.'

'Yes, it is good, because do you know, Mother is quietly thrilled to bits to have him back? And they're getting on like a house on fire.'

'Really? That's fantastic!' I could hardly believe it.

'Mother's a different woman, Lindsey, excited, almost girlish.' He laughed and pushed a hand through his hair, relaxed and easy. 'They've even been making plans for their future,' he added, looking down at his hands which were loosely clasped in front of him. 'And they've decided to sell up and move away from here.'

'Really?' This surprised me enormously, but after I'd thought about it I realised that it was a sensible decision. 'Of course, Amy will live with her mother until John is released, I suppose, 'and Tim will have to manage his own life.' Then I put into words the only drawback I could see. 'Nick, what about you and Emma? Where will you go?'

Nick slid to the floor and walked over to the window. His eyes were on Carn Wartha and his face was serious now. 'It's time for us to make a break as well, Lindsey. Now, before Emma gets settled in school. The dig is finished apart from a few loose ends. There's nothing to keep me here either.'

I nodded. There wasn't anything to add to that. Never in my wildest dreams could I have anticipated what happened next.

Nick reached out a hand, pulled us both to our feet and slipped his arm around my waist. One finger under my chin raised my face to his and our eyes locked as we looked deep into each other's soul. 'I can never repay you for what you've done for Emma and me,' he whispered. He pulled me to him and my head came to rest on his shoulder, which seemed the most natural place for it to be. His breath was warm on my hair as he added, 'You've given me my life back, Lindsey darling.'

I turned my face up to his. 'There's nothing to repay, Nick. I've done what I came here to do.'

At last I was where I'd yearned to be for so long, warm, secure, safe, enfolded in Nick's strong arms. I smiled into that beloved face and his mouth came a little closer. I just closed my eyes and waited for what must surely come now.

'Daddy! Lindsey! What are you doing?' Suddenly the door was flung open and we both jumped and spun round as if we'd been shot. A small figure in blue jeans and an outsize white apron was gazing wide-eyed from the doorway.

Nick and I both burst out laughing, then hand in hand we went forward together to tell Emma the news.

Other titles in the
Linford Romance Library:

THREE TALL TAMARISKS

Christine Briscomb

Joanna Baxter flies from Sydney to run her parents' small farm in the Adelaide Hills while they recover from a road accident. But after crossing swords with Riley Kemp, life is anything but uneventful. Gradually she discovers that Riley's passionate nature and quirky sense of humour are capturing her emotions, but a magical day spent with him on the coast comes to an abrupt end when the elegant Greta intervenes. Did Riley love Greta after all?